‘Cassie?’

Was it her imagination or was there a husky tone to Luke’s voice? There was certainly an extra warmth to the expression in his eyes. ‘I don’t know how to thank you enough for being willing to listen to my tale of woe. I know it hasn’t solved anything, but I think you’ve saved my sanity.’

Suddenly Cassie found herself living one of her forbidden fantasies as Luke stepped forward and wrapped his arms tightly around her.

Her heart stuttered and she completely forgot to breathe after her first startled gasp.

Josie Metcalfe lives in Cornwall now, with her long-suffering husband, four children and two horses, but, as an army brat frequently on the move, books became the only friends who came with her wherever she went. Now that she writes them herself she is making new friends, and hates saying goodbye at the end of a book—but there are always more characters in her head clamouring for attention until she can't wait to tell their stories.

Recent titles by the same author:

COURTING DR CADE
A MILLENNIUM MIRACLE
TAKE TWO BABIES...
A TRUSTWORTHY MAN

ONE AND ONLY

BY

JOSIE METCALFE

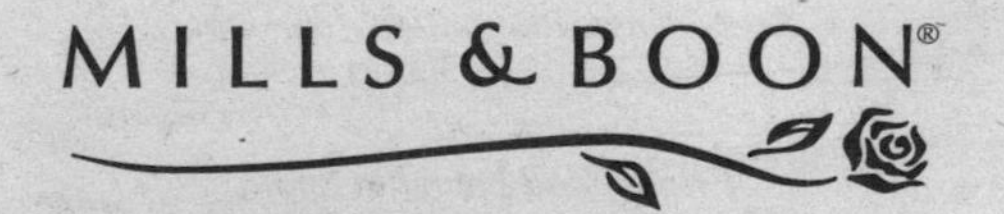

First published in Great Britain 2000
Harlequin Mills & Boon Limited,
Eton House, 18-24 Paradise Road, Richmond, Surrey TW9 1SR

ISBN 0 263 82264 8

Set in Times Roman 10½ on 12 pt.
03-0010-50560

Printed and bound in Spain
by Litografia Rosés, S.A., Barcelona

CHAPTER ONE

'HEY, Cassie, is there any more ice cream left?' demanded a sibilant whisper.

'You had the last of it, Kirstin, *and* the chocolates!' Cassie whispered back and giggled when she heard Naomi's groan in the gloom.

'Does that mean the two of us get to share the rest of the biscuits between us?' she suggested swiftly.

'No way!' Kirstin objected. '*I*'m the one with the sweet tooth. Just because the two of you can eat what you like, without putting on an ounce—'

'Shh!' Cassie warned as the two of them began a tug of war over the packet of chocolate digestives. 'You'll wake everybody up.'

The other two chuckled out loud before they remembered to muffle the sounds. It reminded Cassie of the many times this had happened over the three years since they'd come to live at Dot's. These midnight feasts had been a feature of their relationship since soon after they'd met each other, and they were always getting caught. They might be eighteen years old now, and officially adults, but this time was unlikely to be any different. It didn't seem to matter how quiet they were, Dot always heard what they were up to.

'There are only four of us in the house these days, and three of us are here,' Naomi pointed out with simple logic.

Unlike the first time, when the house had nearly been bursting at the seams, Cassie remembered. The atmosphere in their little torchlit room had been very different that night, filled with fear that they were going to lose each other just when they'd started to form bonds.

'Anyway, I think Dot was expecting us to do this, otherwise why would she have stocked up on all our favourite things?' Kirstin added.

'It *has* become a tradition, this private celebration,' Cassie agreed. 'And with the results of our exams out today, she didn't need to be a mind-reader to guess what we'd do.'

There was silence for a few moments while they all basked in their recent successes. All three of them had donned their night-time 'uniform' of oversized T-shirts and were variously curled and sprawled on Cassie's bed, propped against the wall or headboard.

At their age, they could easily have changed the venue to the comfort of the sitting room, with Dot's blessing, but that wouldn't have followed their tradition. It wouldn't have been the same if they hadn't waited until dark with the secret proceedings lit only by torchlight.

'Well, here's to the next rung up the ladder,' Kirstin announced, holding out the plastic cup of sparkling white wine they had chosen as an affordable substitute for champagne.

'We always said we were going to do it—that if we banded together for support we could make things happen the way we wanted,' Naomi pointed out with smug satisfaction as she stretched out to touch her own cup to the other two. 'Remember? The first time when we had that council of war?'

'How could we forget?' Cassie said softly. 'We'd only been here a few weeks when Dot and Arthur found out that he'd got cancer.'

After their various nightmare experiences *en route* to

this placement in foster care, their arrival at Dot's and Arthur's house had seemed almost too good to be true.

All three of them had been expecting just another version of institutional living but instead had found a real home. The prospect of having it taken away because of Arthur's newly discovered illness had been the spur that had turned the three of them from self-contained individuals into a united force.

'It still makes me smile when I remember the look on that social worker's face,' Cassie murmured reminiscently as she hooked a long strand of blonde hair back over her shoulder.

With hindsight, it had been easy to understand that the poor woman had been at her wit's end. She'd easily managed to find new homes for the last of the younger children in Dot's and Arthur's care. The twins had been orphans and had only arrived a few days earlier. They had been due to leave as soon as their adoptive parents had passed the rigorous scrutiny necessary before taking on such a precious burden.

Trying to place three nearly adult girls in an already overburdened system—especially when those three had already earned themselves reputations as 'difficult' cases—had obviously been a different matter.

Each of them had felt that the social worker hadn't really wanted to place them with Dot and Arthur in the first place—why upset such stalwarts of the fostering system with *three* such horrors?

To have been faced with those same three girls such a short time later and under such tragic circumstances, and to have heard that they'd refused to leave their latest foster home, must have come like a bolt from the blue.

'And Dot cried,' Cassie added, remembering how much the sight of those tears had affected her when she'd been so determined not to care about other people's feelings any more.

'*And* she told the social worker that she wasn't going to let her split us up,' Kirstin recalled. 'She said that we belonged to her now. That we were her family, and that family stood together.'

None of them needed to say anything about the painful months that had followed while, in spite of the best that the hospital could have done, Arthur gradually lost his fight to live. It was no coincidence that all three of 'his girls' had decided on a career in medicine.

'Well, they never managed to split us up *then*, and we aren't being split up *now*,' Naomi pointed out with satisfaction. 'Kirstin might have decided to go one better than the two of us and become a doctor, but we'll all be training at the same place.'

Although their determination could probably have gained the two of them a place at medical school, too, Cassie and Naomi had always been certain that they wanted to concentrate on nursing. Their good exam results today had ensured that all three of them had secured the places they wanted at St Augustine's Hospital.

'It's very satisfying when you get over a hurdle, isn't it?' Cassie murmured as she accepted another biscuit. 'It brings the dreams that much closer.'

She couldn't help remembering the first time the three of them had dared to voice their secret hopes and dreams to each other. It had been several months after they'd come to live with Dot and Arthur and had marked a real milestone in their relationship with each other—the first time they'd really let each other 'inside'.

'Well, look how far we've come already,' Kirstin pointed out. 'When we were sent here, I bet that social worker thought she was going to be spending the next three years watching us go from bad to worse and driving Dot and Arthur mad in the process.'

'She actually apologised to Dot for landing her with three problem cases at once. Especially as they usually didn't take on long-term fostering,' Naomi reminded them. 'Mind you, with our records, they probably didn't think we'd be there more than a couple of days.' If they'd run away, it wouldn't have been the first time for any of them.

In spite of her determination to maintain her emotional isolation, it hadn't taken very long for Dot's and Arthur's brand of gentle persistence to make Cassie realise that she'd fallen on her feet. The other two had obviously been equally affected by the change in their circumstances. Just the threat of being moved away when Arthur had become ill had been enough to fire their determination to do whatever it took to be allowed to stay—even working hard and behaving themselves.

'I don't think my goals have changed so very much, even three years on,' Kirstin volunteered thoughtfully. 'Even then I was determined that as soon as I could I was going to get a good job so I could be independent—so other people couldn't let me down.'

Cassie knew what she meant. All three of them had been let down in one way or another and it had left marks on their characters that would probably endure for a lifetime.

'Over the last three years you've learned to set your sights a little higher,' Naomi pointed out. 'We all have. Do you remember when my ultimate goal was just to be able stay somewhere nice for more than a year?'

'So what is your dream now?' Cassie challenged. 'Today is a milestone in our lives. The day when we can officially say we've achieved our first major goals. We all got the grades we needed to go on to the next stage, so I think it's time we dusted off our dreams again and gave them a bit of a polish.'

'OK. I'll go first,' Kirstin volunteered, flicking a tangle of dark auburn hair back over her shoulder. 'As I said, I was always determined to get myself a good job so I wouldn't have to rely on anyone else for my security. With my medical training, I'll not only have a job for life, and one that lets me do good for others, but it will be something I enjoy.'

'Perhaps you'll even become a consultant,' Cassie suggested loyally, knowing that her friend had the determination to do it if she wanted to. 'What about you, Naomi?' she prompted. 'Are you aiming for the top of the tree, too? Perhaps you'll end up in charge of a whole hospital, not just a ward.'

'Perhaps.' Naomi smiled at the idea. 'But my basic dreams haven't changed very much over the last three years either. I'm still hoping that one day I'll have a real family of my own.'

'Aren't we good enough, then?' Cassie teased, as ever hiding strongly felt emotions behind humour.

'Well, I love you both very much, but only as sisters. I wouldn't want to have your baby,' Naomi joked.

'So, even after everything you went through with your own family, you're still brave enough to want to give it a go?' Kirstin asked quietly, voicing Cassie's secret fears. She knew only too well how devastating it could be for all the members of a family when a marriage went sour.

'Yes,' Naomi answered equally seriously, her hair and eyes very dark in the half-light. 'I'm really looking forward to starting my nursing training, but one day I want to meet someone and fall in love with him and know that I'm the most important person in the world to him.'

'Unfortunately, men don't come with a warranty,' Cassie pointed out wryly, the memories of her own childhood still all too clear. 'If I could be sure that I was going to be the most important person in his world, I might be tempted to take a chance on that particular dream, too.'

She didn't need to remind them of the way her parents had fought in the courts, each one bitterly determined not to be awarded custody. The story had unfortunately been repeated in one foster home after another and, with each disappointment, she'd become more and more disillusioned and impossible to live with.

In spite of the softening effect of the last three years, her friends knew that never again was she going to settle for being second best.

'In the meantime,' she added brightly, 'in case Prince Charming never finds my door, I intend to end up working with the very tiny babies in special care. That's my dream.'

There was a pause of perhaps two seconds before all three of them chanted together, their thoughts having obviously followed the same path.

'"It's all very well having a dream, but if you want it to come true, first you have to wake up…"' they quoted simultaneously, and heard a fourth voice chiming in from the doorway.

'Dot!'

'Caught again!'

'Uh-oh!'

They all laughed as they shuffled across to make room for the diminutive figure approaching the bed. There was no question in any of their minds that the woman who had been a combination of mother, jailer and best friend to all three of them would be warmly welcomed into their midst.

'Well, then,' said Dot when she'd made herself comfortable, her hair a silvery halo of natural curls around her smiling face where the soft torchlight caught it. 'Whose turn is it to try to bribe me this time? And what goodies have you saved for me? It's far too long since the last time I took part in a good midnight feast.'

'There you are, Jiminy Cricket,' Cassie murmured with a last careful caress of the peachskin-like fuzz just starting to cover his head. She hardly dared touch the tissue-fine skin covering bones the same sort of size as a chicken wing. He still looked impossibly small and breakable, even though he'd grown stronger with the passing days and weeks since his premature birth.

'All done, precious. Now I'll leave you in peace so you can have a sleep.' She stripped off her disposable gloves and mask and threw them in the bin.

'Any word from Luke about the situation down in Accident and Emergency?' Melissa asked softly from Neesha's cot a few paces away as she finished changing a tiny disposable nappy on her fragile charge.

'Nothing, as far as I know. Nor from Obs and Gynae.'

She took a quick glance at her watch before she cast a careful look at the displays on the array of monitors surrounding the high-tech cot.

Luke had been due on the unit first thing this morning but had been paged to see an emergency admission almost as he'd arrived for work. They'd checked to make sure that there had been a unit warmed and ready for a new occupant but that had been more than an hour ago and the special care department was still waiting to hear if their expertise was needed.

The main door made its usual swishing sound as it opened and all eyes turned expectantly.

Mr and Mrs Stilliard paused, obviously unnerved by the unusual attention, and their eyes immediately flew towards their precious son.

'Is something the matter?' the young woman asked. 'Has something happened to James?' She had naturally pale skin but as she hurried towards Cassie her face rapidly lost all trace of colour.

'No. He's fine,' Cassie soothed, reaching for her hand and giving it a comforting squeeze. 'In fact, we're really proud of him because he hasn't thrown a single arrhythmia all morning.'

Panic was quickly replaced by relief and beaming delight and Cassie watched the parents cling to each other while they watched James sleep.

Ever since she'd started specialising in the care of premature babies Cassie had needed to come to terms with the fact that the lives of their patients were precariously balanced between success and disaster. It was hard not to become attached to them when she would probably be nursing them through one crisis after another for anything up to twelve hours a day for months on end.

It was wonderful when one of them won the fight and was able to go home to start a normal life, but the constant vigilance could also be extremely wearing on the nerves—as were the times when they lost the battle.

'Sorry I took so long to get here, Cassie,' said a deep voice behind her in the office, startling her out of her thoughts.

She'd been waiting for him to arrive in the department, but even though she'd been trying for the last two years to school her stupid heart into behaving, the sound of Luke's voice still made her pulse give a convulsive leap.

'Problems?' she asked quietly when she saw his expression, hoping her reaction would be taken as concern for a potential patient. He looked drawn and she'd been watching the shadows darkening under his eyes for over a week now. Her heart ached to be able to do something for him.

He shrugged but there was such a wealth of unhappiness in his expression that she suddenly threw caution to the winds.

'Luke, are you sure you didn't come back to work too soon after the accident? You haven't been out of hospital long yourself, and since then the department seems to have been even busier than usual. We're running very close to capacity and you're beginning to look like death warmed up.'

He gave a startled bark of laughter but there was little humour in it.

'Thanks, Cassie. You do my ego a power of good!' He grimaced and added, almost under his breath, 'Everything would be very much easier if work *was* the problem.'

She waited, silently hoping that he was finally going to tell her what was worrying him. She could have groaned aloud when she saw him drag his thoughts back to the job.

'About that call down to Accident and Emergency,' he began, his thoughts obviously on work again. 'As you heard, they had the victims of a car crash on the way in. A pregnant mum likely to deliver her baby prematurely.'

'Someone got their wires crossed?' Cassie was surprised. The new high-tech communication system that St Augustine's had installed meant that the ambulance paramedics were able to talk directly to the hospital from the site of an accident.

'Yes and no.' He sighed. 'The young woman was pregnant but she wasn't far enough along for us to be able to save the child. Only twenty weeks.'

'The baby died?' Cassie asked softly. No wonder Luke seemed so despondent. He hated losing one of 'his' babies.

'They both did,' he confirmed briefly, and rubbed both hands over his face. 'Mother and baby.'

Cassie briefly caught sight of the anguished expression in his eyes before he managed to control it, and she hoped that her own thoughts weren't as readable. Was it the recent events in his own life which were making the situation hit Luke so hard?

'Could you do with a coffee before you catch up on things?' she offered, trying to sound casual. 'The Stilliards are with James and he's been behaving himself this morning so I should have a few minutes to put the kettle on.'

'Coffee would be perfect. Double strength—'

'With one sugar and a splash of milk,' she finished for him. 'If I don't know how you kick-start your system by now...!'

She kept the conversation light as she switched the kettle on, pleased to note the way the tension gradually left him. It also confirmed her belief that the worry weighing him down wasn't something related to work.

She loved her job—it was everything she'd always dreamed it would be—but secretly she had to admit that part of the pleasure for her was working with Luke Thornton. The three months he'd been away from St Augustine's had seemed to stretch on for ever and she hadn't dared to admit to herself how relieved she'd been that he'd recovered well enough from his injuries to return.

She remembered with a shudder the moment when she'd learned about the crash and its awful consequences. She would probably always feel guilty for the fact that she'd all but ignored his wife's tragic death in her relief that Luke had survived.

She gave herself a silent shake to dismiss that pointless train of thought. Luke had obviously never had any idea how much she'd been attracted to him. It seemed as if no sooner had he met her new colleague, Sophie, than the two of them had been married with a baby on the way.

It was her own fault if she still sometimes regretted the fact that she hadn't been the one he'd chosen, but once he'd married she'd forced herself to accept that it was a waste of time pining after him. After her disastrous childhood, she had absolutely no intention of playing second fiddle to anyone, whether in her professional or her private life.

She'd had to work long and hard over the last nine years to achieve her present post on the special care baby unit and she was very happy with the job. It was a pity that her private life hadn't been as successful.

Still, Naomi had found her perfect man and was busily planning her dream wedding, so there was plenty of time for her own Mr Right to come along. And if he didn't, well, she had a career she loved and that was more important to her than to come second best in anyone's estimation.

Cassie suddenly realised that the silence had begun to stretch between them as she'd become lost in her thoughts. She looked up to find Luke's gaze fixed thoughtfully on her, a small frown drawing his tawny brows together.

'What?' she asked, wondering if she'd missed something important. For a moment she was certain that there was a strange expression in his eyes, a look of desolation…or confusion. Whatever it was, it didn't belong in the blue eyes which had once been filled with laughter, but before she could properly analyse it he'd blinked and it was gone…or was it only hidden?

Before either of them could pick up the threads of the conversation there was an insistent shrilling noise and Luke groaned as he fished a small pager out of his pocket.

With a muttered imprecation he strode towards the phone and punched a series of buttons with an impatient finger.

Cassie's heart ached when she picked up on the slight hesitation in his walk, a legacy of the injuries which had kept him on traction up in the orthopaedic department while surgeons had fought to save his leg. He'd been very lucky that he'd only missed three months at work.

'*What?*' Luke exclaimed, the anger in his voice enough to snap Cassie out of her thoughts. 'They can't do that. I won't let them.'

As the call went on, with Luke becoming more and more angry, Cassie realised with a start that it was unlikely to be about hospital business. She was just about to leave the room to give him some privacy when she heard Luke mention lawyers in a harsh tone of voice she'd never heard him use in the past.

He slammed the receiver down.

'Dammit!' he swore, the palm of one hand smacking suddenly against the unforgiving wall beside the phone. 'How dare they? How *dare* they?'

It was the sound of desperation mixed in with the anger that stilled her feet and she turned to face him across the intervening space.

'Luke…?' she began hesitantly, thinking the call must have been about some problem with the ongoing court case resulting from his accident. She'd offered a listening ear not long ago and he hadn't taken her up on it. Why should he do so now?

It was her foolish heart that prompted her to try again.

'Luke, are you sure there isn't anything I can do to help?' she offered softly, directing her words towards the back of his head, held stiffly above a rigid back. 'My ears are fairly fireproof and my shoulders were waterproofed years ago.'

As she watched, she saw him curl his fingers into a white-knuckled fist before he turned to face her. His shoulders hit the wall with a solid thump as he leant back and lifted his eyes to meet hers, and she felt the impact of his misery right to the depths of her soul.

'If only there *were* something you could do,' he muttered hopelessly.

The high-pitched sound of one of the monitors had them both making for the adjoining room, all thoughts of private conversation necessarily put on hold while they found out what was going on.

'Neesha forgot to breathe again,' Melissa reported glumly. 'It only takes a flick of my finger on the bottom of her foot to remind her, but...'

She didn't need to continue. They all knew that it was a signal that Neesha still had a long road to travel before she would be ready for life without extra oxygen and constant supervision.

'How are her observations, apart from that?' Luke asked as he faced Melissa across the cot, his eyes moving alertly over the display on each monitor.

'Pulse is one-fifty, blood pressure seventy over forty and respiration averages sixty-five,' she reported.

'All within normal ranges, even if some are on the high side,' Cassie heard Luke comment quietly.

'When she remembers to breathe,' Melissa added with a wry chuckle.

Cassie couldn't help herself watching the expression on

Luke's face as he looked at the helpless scrap of humanity in the cot in front of him.

He wasn't a particularly large man, probably as much as an inch under six feet, but he was solidly built with the broad shoulders and muscular legs of an active sportsman. But although he looked like a giant beside his frail patient there was nothing but gentleness and concern in his touch as he stroked a careful finger over a set of minute pink toes.

For the rest of her shift it almost seemed to Cassie as if Luke was deliberately avoiding spending time in her company. He was certainly looking more than usually preoccupied and, with the shadowy evidence of strain clear on his face, she found it hard to keep her own thoughts away from him.

She'd resigned herself to the frustration of never finding out what was on his mind, so it came as a surprise when he sought her out as she was preparing to leave.

'Um, Cassie? I was wondering... Have you got plans for this evening?' he began awkwardly.

Rendered almost speechless by the sudden tightness in her throat, she couldn't sort her thoughts out. It almost sounded as if he was trying to ask her out...on a date?

He'd obviously taken her silence for hesitation and hurried on.

'I know it's short notice and your off-duty time is precious, but I've been thinking—about what you said earlier—and I realised that you were right. I do need to talk to someone.'

Cassie didn't know whether to laugh or cry.

On the one hand, she was delighted that, in spite of the slightly uneasy atmosphere between them since he'd been fit enough to return to work, he still felt he could take advantage of their previous friendship to confide his troubles to her. On the other hand, to have her delight at being asked out crushed quite so quickly was a blow.

The trouble was, in spite of the fact that logic told her he could never be the man for her, her heart couldn't help wishing things could have been different.

Still, that was all water under the bridge. She drew in a steadying breath and pinned on a calm expression.

'What time were you thinking of? I've got to go shopping if I'm going to eat tonight and the laundry is starting to inch its own way towards the washing machine, making begging noises.'

'I need to hit the shops, too.' He paused for a moment of thought. 'How about combining forces? If you start with the laundry, I'll come and pick you up when I finish here and provide transport for the shopping trip.'

'It's amazing how much energy you can find when there's an incentive,' Cassie muttered to herself as she took a last glance around the room.

It wasn't large, by any means, and the bedroom was even smaller, barely big enough for the bed, wardrobe and chest of drawers crammed into it. But it was her own private refuge—something she'd craved with a passion after too many years of being forced to share her space with strangers.

And now, after her efforts of the last couple of hours, everything was perfectly clean and tidy. Her second load of laundry should be ready to come out of the tumble-drier as soon as she'd changed out of her scruffy 'house-cleaning' clothes and into something a little less dilapidated.

'Who am I trying to impress?' she scoffed as she started folding her sinfully indulgent underwear and nightdresses into neat piles, in the way Dot had insisted.

'Luke isn't going to be interested in looking for dust bunnies under the furniture.'

As if speaking his name had conjured him up, the buzzer rang right beside her and nearly sent her into orbit.

Suddenly her fingers were all thumbs and when she tried to tuck the incriminating stack out of sight under her arm while she released the catch on the door, it was almost fated that she should drop the lot at his feet.

Luke gazed down in silence at the multi-hued swatches of silky fabric for several achingly long seconds before he looked up with a grin.

'I've heard of strewing someone's path with rose petals but I hadn't heard of this variation on the theme,' he teased, a totally unexpected gleam of mischief in his clear blue eyes.

Cassie didn't know whether to hit him or hug him, but with just one quip he had dispelled all her stupid nerves. Her mishap certainly seemed to have lightened his mood.

He looked so much more relaxed in jeans and a striped rugby shirt, his hair rumpled as though he'd forgotten to comb it after he'd pulled his clothes on. Her fingers itched to smooth down the errant strands but that certainly wouldn't set the right tone for their meeting.

Neither did the array of intimate clothing draped over his trainers.

'Well, don't you dare tread on those because they've just been washed,' she warned as she bent down to scoop them together and carry them out of sight.

It only took a moment to drop the tangled bundle into a drawer with a silent promise to Dot to tidy them as soon as she returned home, then they were on their way.

The shopping trip was much more fun than doing the chore on her own. She teased him about the number of packets of chocolate biscuits he put in his trolley then had to endure teasing of her own when she hung over the ice-cream freezers to make her selection.

'You're only buying that brand because of the sexy adverts,' he challenged, then grabbed a carton of double chocolate for himself.

In spite of the teasing, there was still an air of suppressed tension between them and Cassie was certain it was because they were both thinking about the conversation to come.

'Throw your frozen stuff in with mine,' Luke directed as he began to lob his shopping almost indiscriminately into cupboards and fridge when they returned to his tiny house. 'Then it'll keep till I take you home.'

He switched the kettle on and shoved something into the microwave, before grabbing cutlery and crockery.

Force of habit had Cassie finishing his unpacking and setting the rest of his groceries neatly away. She'd just finished stacking a precarious jumble of tins into some sort of order so that the cupboard door would close properly when she heard the timer on the microwave and realised that Luke had gone very quiet behind her.

She turned to find him watching her with a mixture of amusement and amazement.

'Neat little thing, aren't you? How much would you charge to sort the whole place out? I don't seem to have had time to get straight since I moved in.'

'You couldn't afford the amount I'd have to charge if the rest of it's like this,' she joked, retreating behind humour the way she usually did to hide uncomfortable emotions.

With his reminder that this wasn't the house he'd lived in with Sophie, she hardly thought about the fact that her compulsive tidying was probably overstepping the bounds of polite behaviour.

Theirs had been a much bigger place, just on the outskirts of town and set in a lovely garden, but, according to the hospital grapevine, Luke had apparently sold it while he'd still been in hospital, recovering from his injuries. He'd moved into this place as soon as he'd been released.

'Ah, you're so cruel to me,' he complained melodramatically as he juggled with what he'd taken out of the microwave. 'And after I've slaved for hours over a hot stove to prepare a meal for you.'

He turned and presented her with a plate in the middle of which sat a steaming container of food.

'You and the frozen-food company.' Cassie laughed and accepted his offering. 'Thank you, kind sir, but even such gastronomic delights as this—what is it, by the way? Lasagne? It doesn't entitle you to hours of slave labour to straighten your messy house out.'

By tacit agreement they spent the next few minutes silently clearing their plates, but once the food was gone Luke refilled their coffee-mugs with a decaffeinated brew and sat down again.

Cassie cradled hers between her hands and sat back, a shiver of apprehension snaking up her spine.

'Where to start?' Luke said on a heavy sigh, his eyes following his finger as it trailed round and round the rim of his mug.

'Wherever you like...if you're sure you still want to tell me. And you can stop whenever you want to,' she offered.

'I've got to tell someone or I think I'll go mad,' he said harshly. 'The whole situation is turning into a nightmare.'

CHAPTER TWO

LUKE was silent for several minutes after his outburst, long enough to give Cassie time to regret anew the loss of their easy camaraderie.

It still surfaced at odd moments such as when she teased him about his untidiness or his coffee drinking habits. But even then there seemed to be an air of constraint that made her unable to overstep the invisible line drawn between them.

Where once, not so very long ago, she would have confronted him about his permanent look of preoccupation and worry, now she felt uncomfortable even mentioning it directly.

'Cassie, can I ask you something?' he asked, his voice breaking the uneasy silence, his eyes suddenly very intent.

She gestured for him to go ahead.

'It might sound very self-centred, but, well, I've been wondering… I thought we'd developed a good rapport at work. I thought we were friends. So…why didn't you visit me in hospital?'

Before she could answer, he immediately raised one hand and shook his head. 'You don't have to answer that. I suppose it's egotistical of me to suppose that you'd want to spend your off-duty time in hospital when you work there, too. You'd far rather go out with the latest man in your life.'

'I'm not going out with anyone,' Cassie blurted out, startled into an honest denial by the vulnerable expression he couldn't hide. 'Anyway, that works the other way, too.

I didn't know whether you'd want a visit from someone you see enough of at work. Honestly, it wasn't that I didn't care.'

Far from it, in spite of her best efforts, she thought wryly.

'Anyway,' she continued, slightly defensively, 'I did come to see you, soon after it happened.' She hadn't been able to stay away, needing to see for herself that he really had survived the carnage.

'I don't remember seeing you,' he said with a frown. 'When?'

'You were pretty much out of it,' she admitted ruefully. 'You hadn't been out of surgery long so you were tanked up on painkillers and trussed up like the Christmas turkey.'

'Graphic description!' He grimaced. 'No wonder you didn't want to come back. Visiting me in hospital must have seemed too much like a busman's holiday.'

Cassie didn't answer. She knew that the real reason she hadn't gone back once Luke had been conscious had been her fear that he might have been able to see through her fragile guise of friendship. It had taken the shocking sight of his bruised and battered body to force her to realise that simple determination wasn't going to be enough. In spite of the passage of time, and the fact that he'd been married and had had a child, she hadn't really been able to do more than temporarily stifle her attraction towards him.

She grew uncomfortable under his clear-eyed gaze. Knowing just how intuitive he could be when dealing with one of their little patients, she didn't like to think how easily he might be able to analyse *her* feelings.

'So...are you going to tell me what's going on?' she

asked, hoping to set his thoughts off onto another track. 'Is it a problem with the court case?'

He frowned and she became slightly defensive, wondering if he was displeased that she should know about his private business.

If she were honest she would have to admit that she'd been unable to stop herself gleaning every bit of hospital gossip about the event that she could. It seemed that it was common knowledge that the person who had lost control and ploughed into their car almost head-on had killed Sophie outright and had nearly maimed Luke for life because he'd been concentrating on talking into his mobile phone. It had been a miracle that their little daughter had emerged virtually unscathed.

'Well, it was reported at the time, so everyone has heard that the driver who caused the crash is being prosecuted. And then, today, I couldn't help overhearing you mention lawyers on the phone.'

'That court case is the *least* of my worries,' he said dismissively. 'It's Sophie's parents that are the problem now.'

'The ''in-laws from hell''?' she quoted, reminding him of an earlier indiscreet criticism of the couple in question. Cassie had met them briefly both at Luke's and Sophie's wedding and at Jenny's christening and had noticed that the couple had seemed excessively concerned with keeping up appearances.

'I thought you'd declared a truce with them since they became grandparents?' she continued. 'Haven't they been looking after Jenny while you've been in hospital?'

'That's the problem,' Luke admitted heavily, his expression a mixture of anger and despair. 'Now they seem to have got the idea that she should be their replacement for the daughter they lost. They've decided they want to keep her.'

'You're going to fight them,' Cassie said swiftly, not even bothering to make it a question.

The very idea that he would allow someone to take his child away was unthinkable. She'd known Luke for more than two years now, and knew how much he loved children—especially the perfect little daughter he and Sophie had created between them.

She was shocked that, after all he'd lost, his in-laws could even think of threatening Luke with something so cruel.

Inside her a maelstrom of emotion roiled and churned. She was envious of both the relationship he'd had with Sophie and his protectiveness towards his little daughter. Luke would fight to have Jenny with him while her own father had done everything he could have to avoid the responsibility.

Most of all she was jealous of the fact that Luke's child existed, and she'd found herself wishing many times that Jenny could have been *their* child.

'Of course I'm going to fight,' Luke vowed, his blue eyes fierce and with a pugnacious set to his jaw. 'She's my daughter and I'll do anything I have to.'

'Luke, you don't need to come in with me. I can manage,' Cassie insisted as she tried to take the rest of her shopping bags from him. She was worried that he might be overstressing his recently healed leg, but she might as well have saved her breath.

'This was part of the deal,' Luke said stubbornly as he swung the plastic carriers out of her reach. 'I've spent the evening talking your ears off so the least I can do is make certain you and your shopping arrive home safely.'

With innate courtesy he held the front door open for her with an outstretched elbow then accompanied her up the stairs.

It all felt so wonderfully domestic and ordinary, she realised suddenly. As though the two of them were a married couple returning home after doing the week's shopping.

Except that they weren't any sort of a couple, married or otherwise, she reminded herself sternly as she led the way into her pocket-sized kitchen.

'Just put them in the corner beside the fridge, thanks,' she said as she extracted the frozen stuff and stacked it straight in the freezer section. 'I'll put it all away in a minute.'

'You're sure you don't want me to help? After all, you helped me with mine.'

'No, thanks! I'd rather be able to find things when you've gone,' she teased, slightly breathless when she realised just how much space he took up.

He'd pushed the sleeves of the rugby shirt up his arms and the light was striking golden gleams on the fine, dark hairs, tempting her to touch them to find out if they really were as silky as they looked.

This early in the summer, his skin was still winter pale, especially after his long stay in traction, and she could see the fading evidence of the myriad cuts and gouges which had shocked her so much when she'd seen him after the accident.

'Cassie?' Was it her imagination or was there a husky tone to Luke's voice? There was certainly an extra warmth to the expression in his eyes. 'I don't know how to thank you enough for being willing to listen to my tale of woe. I know it hasn't solved anything, but I think you've saved my sanity.'

Suddenly Cassie found herself living one of her forbidden fantasies as Luke stepped forward and wrapped his arms tightly around her.

Her heart stuttered and she completely forgot to breathe after her first startled gasp.

He was so big and strong, his body radiating warmth everywhere it touched hers from the lean length of his thighs to the velvety rasp of his jaw against her cheek.

Her pulse began to race, or could it be his heartbeat she could feel? Was he as affected as she was by their first intimate contact? Could this be the start of a new era in their relationship?

'I needed this, Cassie,' he murmured softly, his warm breath on the side of her neck sending shivers of awareness up and down her spine. 'Thank you for being such a good friend.'

Friend?

Cassie pulled the covers up over head and screamed silently.

She'd nearly made a complete fool of herself. There she'd been, with her common sense floating off in a happy pink haze, imagining all sorts of impossibly romantic scenarios, when all Luke had been doing had been giving her a hug to thank her for listening to his problems.

Thank goodness she was accustomed to working under pressure. At least it had enabled her to make some sort of calmly dismissive reply while she'd showed him out of her door.

Now it was time to get her head in order. She would be seeing him again in the morning and they would be working together as usual. There must be nothing in her reaction to him to let him think anything had changed with that spontaneous embrace.

Because, in truth, nothing had changed. He was still Luke Thornton with a child he adored and a wife he had loved and lost. She was still Cassie Mills, determined that the man she gave her heart to would be equally as willing to give his to her in return.

Cassie paused outside the hospital's main entrance and drew in a last deep breath.

The sight of the early morning sunshine when she'd opened her curtains had prompted her to opt for walking to work today.

Apart from the fact that she hadn't slept particularly well, she'd felt the need for the sort of solitude that a brisk walk offered.

She'd also needed the time to make certain that her thoughts were in order. In the wake of those few seconds in Luke's arms, her dreams had taken an unexpectedly lurid turn. It was important that she reminded herself that, stupid dreams or not, he only saw her as a friend.

'Thank goodness you're early,' Carolyn exclaimed as Cassie arrived on the ward. Being her opposite number, they usually only got to see each other for a few brief minutes during handover. 'Joan had to go home early because of a family emergency and Farah's just phoned to say she won't be coming into work today. She was sick earlier this morning and daren't bring any infection into the unit. *And* we're waiting for a post-operative case to arrive.'

Cassie applauded Farah's prudent decision to stay at home, even though it would temporarily cause chaos.

'Have they managed to reach anyone to cover for her shift?'

'Personnel promised to phone back in a minute to let us know. We're coping at the moment, but only just.'

'Who's in surgery? Not one of ours?' Cassie's eyes had automatically done a quick sweep of the unit and couldn't see any empty spaces.

'No, not one of ours, thank goodness.' They all grew very attached to 'their' babies. 'It's a three-week-old small-for-dates with intussusception,' Carolyn detailed succinctly. 'He came in as an emergency during the night.'

Cassie raised her eyebrows. 'That's very young to have that happen. It's far more likely around weaning.'

Carolyn shrugged. 'Apparently, he was in a very bad state by the time he was brought into A and E. I've put the relatives in the little interview room with a tray of tea and a junior while they're waiting for him to arrive on the ward.'

'How are they? Has anyone had time to explain what's happening?'

'I started to, but I wasn't getting anywhere. The mother burst into tears and said it was all her fault, and the mother-in-law was glowering and muttering.'

'Are the admission details on the computer? As I'm officially an extra body until my shift starts, perhaps I could go and have a word with them before he arrives here from Theatre. They'll need a bit of preparation before they see him with all those tubes.'

Carolyn waved her off with grateful thanks and a promise to hold the fort until she came back. 'And I'll give Personnel a quick reminder that we're waiting for reinforcements before the night shift are due to disappear.'

Cassie accessed Matthew Bradley-Whyte's admission notes and jotted the salient facts in the little notepad she carried in her pocket. Then she followed that up with a quick phone call to get the latest update on his condition.

A quick glance at her watch told her that she still had

ten minutes before she was due to sign on. In any case, Carolyn knew where she was.

'Mrs Bradley-Whyte?' Cassie began when she'd tapped on the door and had let herself in. She nodded silently to the junior nurse who slipped quietly out of the room with evident relief.

The two women left in the room couldn't have been more different. The older woman was vast and decked in something that resembled a flower-sprinkled tent, but an obviously expensive tent—a marquee, perhaps. Her face was exquisitely if heavily made up and she didn't have a hair out of place. Her companion, on the other hand, looked as though she had spent the last week or two going through hell, her slender body looking positively gaunt draped in a shapeless maternity dress.

'Yes,' snapped the older woman, completely drowning her younger companion's voice. 'I'm Mrs Bradley-Whyte.'

Cassie couldn't help it, but her hackles rose. It was understandable that relatives would be worried when such a young child was involved, but there was something about the large woman's self-important attitude that immediately rubbed her up the wrong way.

'Are you Matthew's mother?' she challenged in a studiously polite voice.

'Of course not. I'm his grandmother,' she snapped. 'And I want to know why I've been shut in here without so much as—'

'Then *you* must be the Mrs Bradley-Whyte I'm looking for,' Cassie interrupted without a qualm as she perched on the settee beside the younger woman and offered her hand. 'I'm Sister Cassie Mills and I'm on the staff here in the special care baby unit.'

'H-hello,' she whispered, her hand visibly shaking as

it came out to meet Cassie's and clung convulsively. 'Please…have you seen Matthew? Is…is he all right?'

Cassie smiled and gave the trembling hand a reassuring squeeze. Where the poor woman's face wasn't pale and drained, it was blotchy and swollen with the evidence of tears and her eyes were full of fear.

'I've just spoken to someone up in Theatre. The operation's over now, and Matthew's in the recovery room. They should be bringing him down to us in just a little while.'

'Is…is he going to be all right?' she asked hesitantly. 'He's not going to die?'

'The operation went well and there's every chance that he'll make a complete recovery with only the scar to remind you.'

'Scar?' interrupted the older woman sharply, proving that she'd been following every word. 'What sort of scar? Where? Is he going to be disfigured? For heaven's sake, the child only had a stomach upset. Probably not getting enough food, he's so puny.' She sniffed and folded self-righteous arms under a bust the size of an over-stuffed bolster.

'Excuse me, Mrs Bradley-Whyte,' Cassie said quietly, holding onto the younger woman's hand and her temper. 'The doctor confirmed that what Matthew was suffering from wasn't just a tummy-ache but an ileocaecal intussusception.'

'Is that very serious?' the younger woman asked. 'When we brought him in he looked so ill. He kept screaming with pain and pulling his little knees up, but when he went quiet he was all pale and sweaty and he's been very sick. And there was blood and some red gooey stuff in his nappy…a bit like redcurrant jelly.'

'The doctor will be able to give you all the details but,

yes, Matthew could easily have died if you hadn't brought him in when you did.'

She retrieved her hand to take out her trusty notepad and flipped to a fresh page where she started to sketch an explanatory diagram. 'It's very rare in a baby as young as Matthew, but what happened is that part of his intestine had started telescoping inside the rest and caused a blockage—a bit like when you take off a pair of rubber gloves and a finger turns inside out.'

'How do they get it to go the right way again?' She was examining the drawing closely and Cassie could see that her interest in the mechanics of the situation had started to override her natural fear.

'If the problem is brought in straight away it can often be corrected without surgery, but once the tissues have been constricted like that for any length of time they start to deteriorate. Then surgery is essential.'

'How much of his insides have they taken away? Will he be able to eat normally? I only started feeding him cereal a few days ago.'

'Cereal?' Cassie's antennae went on the alert. 'But he's only three weeks old. Why would he be having cereal yet?'

'Because the child's so small and underweight, of course,' Mrs Bradley-Whyte broke in scornfully. 'She's got to get some weight on him somehow or he's never going to amount to anything.'

Cassie drew in a breath and prayed for patience. The only thing she could do was try to ignore the wretched woman and concentrate on the young mother.

'And have you been able to feed him yourself or is he having bottles?' Once again, Cassie had directed her question to Matthew's mother, but that didn't deter the older woman.

'Feeding him herself, more's the pity,' she scoffed. 'At least with a bottle you know how much he's having and you can add an extra spoonful of formula to give his tummy something to work on.'

Cassie bit the tip of her tongue and silently counted to five. She thought she'd done it surreptitiously but a sudden quirk of a hitherto unhappy mouth drew her attention up to meet the younger woman's knowing eyes.

'And you're still feeding Matthew yourself?' she asked, still trying to act as though the interfering woman hadn't spoken...to no avail.

'Well, she'll have to give up now, won't she?' she decreed categorically. 'She can hardly continue while the child's in hospital.' The tone of the strident pronouncement suddenly reminded Cassie of Luke's 'in-laws from hell' and she resolved to tell this young woman about their joint membership in the exclusive club at the earliest opportunity.

'If you like,' Cassie continued with carefully feigned equanimity—the ignorant woman was *not* going to make her lose her cool, 'we can arrange for the use of a breast pump so you can draw the milk off. That way you can keep the supply going for when Matthew's ready to take normal feeds. He could be on a drip for several days but, depending on the scale of the operation, he might be ready for oral feeding in as little as twelve hours. There'd be no problem about using up any of your spare milk because we've always got tiny babies who need the real thing.'

It was such a shame that, instead of being browbeaten by her harridan of a mother-in-law, the new mother hadn't thought to contact the midwife attached to her local doctor's surgery for advice. It might have saved her all this worry.

'How...how much *have* they cut away?' she asked, and Cassie realised that she'd been distracted by the topic of cereal and hadn't answered her question the first time.

'That's something only the surgeon can tell you, but it's usually just the damaged section. Once he's recovered from the operation, Matthew should be as good as new. Not right away, of course,' she added hastily, not wanting to raise her hopes too far, too fast. 'He's had major surgery so he won't be very happy, but once his temperature and the swelling in his tummy goes down he should start improving in leaps and bounds.'

She had just started explaining briefly about the role of the nasogastric tube and the IV lines, which they should expect to see, when there was a brief tap at the door.

'Doctor!' Mrs Bradley-Whyte exclaimed theatrically when she caught sight of Luke in a fresh set of surgical greens. With a turn of speed that startled Cassie, the woman was out of her seat and surging across the room like a galleon in full sail.

Luke accorded her a distantly polite smile but side-stepped and made directly for the young woman once more hanging very tightly onto Cassie's hand.

'Mrs Bradley-Whyte, I'm Luke Thornton,' he said as he perched on the arm of the nearest chair and offered his hand. 'I've just accompanied Matthew from the recovery room down to the unit. As soon as he's settled in you can go through and see him.'

'Please, is he going to be all right?' she pleaded, and Cassie saw the way Luke's expression softened at the sight of her distress.

'He's going to have several rough days before you'll be able to see that he's really on the mend.' He paused and glanced at Cassie. Somehow she knew that he was asking whether she thought the young woman would want to know the details and she gave him the go-ahead with an infinitesimal nod of her head.

'Unfortunately,' he continued seriously, 'a section of his intestines had already become gangrenous and that meant—'

'Gangrenous!' repeated the senior Mrs Bradley-Whyte in horrified tones. 'My grandson has gangrene? Oh, my God!'

Cassie resorted to biting her tongue again but Luke had no such compunction.

'Madam,' he said in quelling tones, glaring at her as she hovered over them like some malevolent floral storm-cloud, 'I am having an important conversation with the mother of my patient. If you cannot control your hysteria you will have to leave.'

'Leave?' she repeated, her voice rising towards an unattractive shriek. 'How dare you? I'm not hysterical and I'm not leaving. You can't make me leave.'

'Oh, but, madam, I can,' he countered, without once raising his voice. 'It would just take one phone call from me to have you escorted from hospital premises...by the police, if necessary.'

Cassie didn't know if that was strictly true but, seeing the way her eyes boggled, it had certainly given the woman something to think about.

'But...but I'm the child's *grandmother*,' she announced self-importantly, obviously still determined to battle it out.

'That's right,' Luke agreed with a gentle smile that didn't match the steely glint Cassie could see in his eyes. 'You're *only* the grandmother, whereas this lady is the patient's *mother*. If you have any position here it is purely to act as support for her. If you can't manage that, then you have no place in my department.'

There were several seconds of deathly silence and Cassie was almost certain that at least three of them in the room were holding their breath.

'Well!' she huffed, very obviously put out by his quiet adamance and determined that they should all know it. 'I've never in all my life been so...' She must have seen something in Luke's expression because she subsided rapidly into a less than dignified silence and sat herself down with a bad-tempered thump.

'As I was saying,' Luke continued imperturbably, 'because a section of his intestines had become gangrenous, it had to be removed and then the two healthy ends were sewn back together. It could be three days before he's ready for his first feed by mouth but I'm confident that we'll soon have him fighting fit.'

There was another tap at the door and the junior stuck her head round at Luke's invitation to tell him that Matthew was ready for his first visitor.

Mrs Bradley-Whyte, senior, leapt to her feet and was already halfway to the door before she noticed Luke holding his hand out, palm towards her like a traffic policeman.

'Just a minute,' he requested, before addressing the younger woman. 'It would probably make things a lot easier all round if we could find some way to differentiate between the two Mrs Bradley-Whytes.'

The younger of the two responded first with a hesitant smile. 'Please, would it be permissible for you to call me Clare?'

'Perfectly, if you're the one giving the permission,' he said with an answering smile. 'Right, then, Clare, do you also give your permission for Mrs Bradley-Whyte to go in with you to visit Matthew?'

Cassie watched the young woman blink and wondered

if it was the first time she'd ever had any power over the wretched steamroller of a woman.

'How long will we be allowed to stay with him?' she asked warily. 'Will it only be for a few minutes shared between the two of us?'

'Nothing like that,' he reassured her. 'You'll gradually be learning how to help the nurses with his care so you'll be allowed to stay with him for most of the time—at least until we throw you out to go and get some sleep,' he added with a hint of a grin. 'As for other visitors, they can only stay as long as they don't make a nuisance of themselves with you or the staff. After all, every child in the unit is seriously ill and doesn't need unnecessary disturbance.'

Cassie was hiding a grin of her own as she led the two of them towards Matthew's special cot. It had certainly taken the mother-in-law from hell down a peg or two to have to be given permission to visit by her lowly daughter-in-law.

Once she'd introduced them to Karen, the nurse who would be specialling Matthew in the first hours after his operation, she made her excuses and went to join Carolyn.

'I'm sorry to make you so late,' she said as she hurried into the tiny office. 'I had no idea that little party would go on so long.'

'Rather you than me,' her colleague said. 'I could hear the mother-in-law sounding off halfway across the unit.'

Cassie briefly detailed her suspicions that the inexperienced young woman had been browbeaten into pushing solid food into her baby long before his system had been ready.

'She's probably going to have some attacks of guilt over the next few days, thinking that she nearly killed her own baby just because she wouldn't stand up against the old battleaxe. She'll need plenty of support,' she concluded.

'Especially when that battleaxe recovers from her put-down and starts trying to throw her weight around again,' Carolyn added wryly. 'Shall we get this handover done before anything else comes along to stop me going home?'

With Matthew in the unit they were running even closer to capacity, their little patients ranging from an emergency premature Caesarean, necessitated by the onset of eclampsia, through several with life-threatening birth defects of the heart or other internal organs.

All the babies went through good days and bad days and this one would probably be no different, but it was the successful release of a child who had come to them with little chance of life that was the reason she loved her job so much.

'By the way,' Carolyn added on her way out of the door, 'Personnel rang back to say they didn't have a single member of staff available for the start of this shift.'

'What?' Cassie exclaimed, horrified. 'We can't be expected to run a high staff ratio department like this without the right number of staff. It's too dangerous.'

'That's why they're sending *two* along in about half an hour,' Carolyn finished with a smug grin. 'Will that do?'

'You rat! You deliberately let me think that we were going to be short-staffed.'

'It's just so easy to rattle your chain, Cassie. All I have to do is make you believe someone isn't treating your precious babies right…' Her voice faded away down the corridor as she gave a cheeky wave over one shoulder.

Cassie had to chuckle. Carolyn was right. The thought that her patients might be at risk was something she couldn't countenance. There was too thin a line between success and disaster to take chances.

The phone by her elbow gave a shrill ring and she picked it up smartly. For the next eight hours this was her domain and there would be no disasters in the unit if there was anything she could do to avoid it.

'Special Care Baby Unit. Sister Cassie Mills speaking. Can I help you?'

'This is Sam Dysart over on Obs and Gyn. I'm trying to reach Luke Thornton to give him a message. Do you know where he's got to?'

Cassie glanced up out of the wide glass panels that gave her an unobstructed view of the ward from her desk.

Luke was on the far side of the room, talking to the parents of a five-week-old girl who had needed major reconstructive heart surgery to correct a life-threatening abnormality. It looked as if the discussion was a serious one and she would rather not interrupt if it was avoidable.

'Is it urgent? He's with a patient at the moment. Can I give him a message or would you rather that he phoned back?'

'If you could give him a name and a number for me that would be a big help. Tell him it's the solicitor we were talking about this morning in the theatre changing room.'

Cassie wrote the number down in her trusty notepad and had barely hung the phone up when Luke joined her in the office.

'Baby Helen's doing well,' he announced with a satisfied smile. 'And her parents look at least ten years younger this morning.'

'It never ceases to amaze me how well the human body bounces back if it's given half a chance,' she agreed then tore out the sheet of paper from her notebook and held it out to him. 'Sam Dysart just phoned through this name and number. He said it's the man you were talking about this morning.'

Luke's smile disappeared as he took the note and Cassie had a horrible sinking feeling when she saw the look of strain that replaced it.

'Luke...' she hesitated a moment, not certain whether their conversation last night gave her the right to ask questions, then plunged on regardless. 'Luke, he said it's the name of a solicitor. They're not really going to go through with it, are they? They're not going to take your little girl away?'

CHAPTER THREE

'THEY'RE *not* going to take my daughter away because I'm not going to let them,' Luke declared with quiet determination.

Cassie felt her heart swell with something that felt suspiciously like pride. She saw the same air of resolve about him each time a new patient came under his care, and knew that it just wasn't in him to give up until he had tried everything to achieve his aim.

'It just seems so unfair!' she exclaimed suddenly. 'After all you've been through over the last few months and then to have *this* hanging over you.'

'Whatever made you think that life was meant to be fair?' he asked simply. 'Just take a look through that window and tell me what's fair about the pain and suffering each one of those little mites is going through. What did they ever do to deserve that?'

'Absolutely nothing,' she agreed quickly. 'Of course, you're right. They're just innocent victims of chance...but I still can't understand how your in-laws can reconcile their loss with stealing your daughter.'

'That's because your brain works in an honest, straightforward way and expects the rest of the world to do the same.' He gazed intently at her for several seconds, almost as though he were trying to see right inside her head.

'What?' she challenged, feeling strangely vulnerable to such close examination. It was a good job she knew he *couldn't* read her mind.

'You're a very all-or-nothing person,' he pronounced suddenly.

Cassie felt a prickle of awareness run over her skin, raising all the tiny hairs. If he knew that much about her, perhaps he *did* know what she was thinking.

'In what way?' she hedged.

'Lots of ways.' He waved an expressive hand, gesturing to include the whole department. 'I can remember you telling me about your decision to become a children's nurse. Being you, you threw yourself into it heart and soul until you got exactly where you wanted to be.'

Her cheeks grew warm at the unsolicited testimonial and she was definitely beginning to regret initiating the conversation. This was supposed to be about his conflict with his in-laws.

Unfortunately, before she could recover her tongue fast enough to change the topic, he was speaking again.

'I wouldn't be surprised if you carried that trait into every aspect of your life,' he continued, musing aloud. 'I know you've maintained your friendship with Naomi over on Paediatrics and Kirstin on Obs and Gyn ever since you first met as teenagers. I'm only surprised you haven't put that same single-mindedness into acquiring a family of your own. Your husband certainly couldn't complain if you put that much effort and dedication into a marriage.'

'I'd like to think that'll be the case,' she replied rather stiltedly, inwardly wishing that someone would rescue her from her embarrassment. 'But first I've got to find Mr Right.'

Why didn't the phone ring? Why did no one want her help? Why didn't the ground open up and swallow her?

'And how will you know that he's Mr—or even Dr—Right?' he challenged swiftly.

'When I find someone with the same goals as mine.

Someone who's willing to put just as much effort into the relationship as I am. Someone who will see me as the one and only person who can make his life complete.'

She'd startled herself with the speed of her reply, almost as if the answer had been there, ready and waiting on the tip of her tongue. Perhaps it *had* been. After all, she'd been thinking about her own prospects of marriage ever since Naomi had announced her engagement several months ago.

If she'd startled herself with her fervent reply it seemed as if she'd surprised Luke even more if the speculative expression in his eyes was anything to go by. For a moment she thought he was going to debate the point further but then an almost visible curtain descended to leave his face expressionless.

He straightened up from his perch on the corner of the desk. 'Best of luck with finding him,' he muttered with a wry expression and a shake of his head. 'Although I think you'd do better to pray for a miracle,' he added pessimistically on his way out of the office.

'Cynic,' she threw after him, and had the satisfaction of hearing him chuckle at the charge.

There was no time to ponder their conversation as it was time to get one of their little charges ready for her trip upstairs to Theatre.

Victoria Ford was the daughter of one of Kirstin's patients, an otherwise healthy full-term baby girl who'd had the misfortune to be born with both a harelip and a cleft palate.

Unfortunately, the defects were so severe that the poor child was unable to suckle properly even with a special prosthesis in position. Her consequent failure to thrive was the reason she was being operated on so soon after birth.

'I can't think what I might have done,' Cathy Ford said tearfully as she cradled the infant in her arms. 'Tom looked cleft palate up in our medical encyclopaedia at home and it said that it happened to her when I was only seven weeks pregnant. But I never take any drugs, not even aspirin, so I wouldn't have taken anything like that dreadful thalidomide, and nothing like this has ever happened in either of our families before so it can't be inherited.'

'Shh,' Cassie soothed. 'Getting yourself all upset isn't going to help Victoria. She needs you to be calm and loving before she goes up to Theatre.'

'I'm sorry.' She sniffed and fished one-handed in her dressing-gown pocket looking for a handkerchief. 'I know you're right and I do love her, in spite of the fact that she isn't the perfectly pretty baby we were expecting.'

'You wait until you see her when all the bandages come off,' Cassie promised. 'She'll still have those beautiful blue eyes and long dark lashes, but you'll hardly recognise the rest of her face. It'll seem like magic.'

Cathy Ford looked unconvinced as she gazed down at the face which was a travesty of all those pretty cherub baby pictures on the congratulation cards.

As if on cue, Victoria began to cry, making the misshapen hole taking up the middle of her face seem more grotesque than ever.

'What's the matter with her? Is she in pain?' the nervous young mother demanded.

'Nothing like that.' Cassie smiled. 'She's just letting you know that because she's due in Theatre in a few minutes she had to miss her last feed and her tummy's empty.'

'Oh.' She smiled in return. It was a rather wobbly effort but it was better than the threat of more tears.

Her daughter cried again, her perfect little chin quivering as she wailed her disapproval, and Cassie saw something indefinable change in the way Cathy Ford was holding her baby.

'Don't cry, precious,' she murmured, apparently forgetting for a moment that Cassie was even there as she cradled the unhappy mite a little tighter and began to rock her. 'I know you're hungry, but in a few minutes you'll be going to sleep and when you wake up it'll all be over.'

She glanced quickly up at Cassie and down again at the fretting baby.

'I was wondering...after the operation... I'd always intended to feed her myself but she couldn't suck. Will I be able to try again after the operation or will my milk have dried up?'

'She won't be able to feed straight away after the operation but we can certainly tube-feed her your breast milk until she's ready. And that will keep your supply going.'

Tom Ford arrived to complete the family group just as the message arrived from Theatre that it was time for Victoria to go up.

Cassie gave a sigh of relief as she saw them leave the unit. Tom had been entrusted with the job of carrying his little daughter while Cathy chatted nervously with Pamina, the staff nurse who would be specialling Victoria when she returned to the ward.

Tom and Cathy had leapt at the chance to wait with their daughter until the anaesthetist had put her to sleep. Cassie hadn't met a parent yet who didn't want to give just one last kiss and a whispered 'I love you' to their precious child.

Then, if they didn't go to find something to eat, the two of them would probably return to the unit to wait in the parents' room until the operation was over. At least the surroundings were familiar, while the waiting room up by the theatres was like alien territory.

But it would probably be several hours before it was time for the unit to take over responsibility for the baby's recovery, and in the meantime there were always a thousand and one things that needed doing.

Cassie was woken by a shrill buzzing and turned over with a muttered imprecation.

Without opening her eyes, she reached out to flap her hand at the alarm clock but it wouldn't stop buzzing.

'I don't believe it,' she groaned as she struggled to sit up and investigate the problem. 'My first lie-in for weeks and my alarm clock goes on the blink.'

The buzz came again and she suddenly realised that it wasn't the alarm clock she was hearing but someone leaning on the buzzer for the front door.

'This had better not be a door-to-door salesman,' she grumbled as she staggered over to the recently installed intercom box. 'And if it's Naomi with another batch of possibilities for bridesmaid's dresses…'

She stabbed the button viciously.

'H'lo,' she mumbled round a yawn, her finger slipping off the button almost before she'd finished speaking.

'Cassie? I'm sorry… Did I wake you up? It's Luke.'

She knew it was Luke. Every cell in her body knew it was Luke as soon as she heard his voice, and suddenly she wasn't the tiniest bit sleepy any more.

'Uh, Cassie, if I've caught you at a bad time, I could always—'

'No!' Now she couldn't get her finger on the button fast enough. 'No, it's quite all right. I'm up but I was just…just lazing around a bit as it's my late morning.'

'Well, I'm sorry if I'm intruding, only I've just had a meeting with that solicitor and—'

'Luke.' She cut him off, realising that it was stupid for them to be talking via the intercom like this. 'When you hear the buzzer, push the front door open and come on up. I'll leave my door on the latch for you to come in.'

She pressed the second button to release the security catch on the main front door then whirled to give her tiny flat an all-encompassing examination.

Thank goodness she wasn't someone who could bear living in a mess. It might make her seem fussy, but at least it was always tidy enough to receive visitors. That meant that she had about one minute to do something about her lack of clothing before Luke would be walking through her door.

'Cassie?' she heard as she grabbed a handful of underwear, still standing there in one of the skimpiest nightdresses she owned. What had the wretched man done—run all the way up the stairs?

'I'll be with you in a minute. Do you want to put the kettle on?' she called as she abandoned the underwear and reached for the white silk wrap Naomi and Kirstin had given her for her last birthday.

There wasn't time to get dressed and, anyway, she wouldn't really have felt right about stripping off her nightdress while Luke was wandering about in her private space.

She dragged a brush quickly through the tangled skeins of her shoulder-length hair, grimacing as she hit a stubborn knot, then hurriedly secured the white wrap firmly over the pale peach of her nightdress.

'Tea or coffee?' Luke asked, obviously having heard her when she arrived in the doorway in spite of her bare feet.

'Coffee, please,' she said fervently. 'I'm beginning to think I'm addicted to that first cup in the morning.'

'Two coffees, coming up.' He turned towards her with a mug in each hand and promptly dropped both of them when he caught sight of her. 'Good God, Cassie, are you wearing anything under that thing?'

She glanced down at herself and suddenly realised that her peach nightdress was probably all but invisible under the white wrap.

'Of course I am,' she retorted indignantly, but the very idea that he'd thought she was almost naked in front of him had heat searing up her throat and into her face as she wrapped both arms around herself.

She whirled away from him and beat a hasty retreat, calling over her shoulder, 'I'll leave you to clear the mess up and make another coffee while I throw some clothes on.'

Her hands were shaking as she tried to concentrate on putting her underwear on without falling over. She absolutely refused to think about the strange electric heat that had instantaneously flooded through her in response to his reaction.

He was an observant man. What if he'd noticed the effect he'd had on her body? He couldn't have missed the way she'd blushed but had he also seen the way her pulse and breathing had gone haywire and her nipples had blatantly pressed against the flimsy fabrics she was wearing?

She covered her face and groaned. If it hadn't been for the fact that she wanted to hear about Luke's meeting with the solicitor, she would have been tempted to lock herself in the bathroom until he gave up waiting and went away.

As it was, she didn't know whether the news was good

or bad, and the fact that she'd never been so embarrassed in her life wasn't a good enough reason for denying Luke the support he needed.

Go out there and pretend it didn't happen, she told herself when she'd donned jeans and a delft blue shirt. He's enough of a gentleman not to say anything—not that there was anything wrong with what I had on. It only *looked* as if I wasn't wearing a nightdress.

Except when she walked out into the sitting room he didn't need to say anything to let her know what he was thinking. All it took was one glimpse of the searing heat in his dark eyes as they travelled the length of her fully clothed body and she knew.

Then he shuttered his gaze and gestured towards the second cup waiting for her on the corner of the table. Cassie slid onto the far end of the settee and eagerly buried her nose in the brew for a sustaining sip.

She fixed her eyes on the gently steaming mug in a vain attempt at keeping them away from where they wanted to be—taking a similar appreciative look at every inch of the powerful body occupying the other end of her settee.

Before the silence could grow uncomfortable she drew in a steadying breath and forced herself to speak.

'So what did the solicitor have to say? Has he been able to get in contact with your in-laws? Are they going ahead with it?'

She dared a glance in his direction and found him equally engrossed in his coffee with a dark expression on his face.

'He hasn't been able to speak to their solicitor yet, so I don't know whether they're going ahead or not. In the meantime, he was able to go through a few things with me to prepare me in case it does come to a court battle.'

'What sort of things?' Her heart ached for his unhappiness. She could only imagine how helpless he must be feeling.

'He's dealt with custody disputes before and knows some of the tricks—like trying to dig up evidence to prove that I'm not a fit person to bring a child up.'

'Well, they're bound to fail if they try to do that,' she scoffed. 'Who could be better than a specialist in paediatrics?'

He glanced up at her with a cynical expression on his face. 'Unfortunately, they also take into account things such as my financial situation, my degree of disability after the accident and my timetable and workload. It doesn't help my case if they can say that I'm too busy to be able to spend enough time with her.'

'Well, you might not be earning a fortune but it must be ample for taking care of one little girl, otherwise every doctor in the country would have to be single and celibate,' she declared staunchly. 'As for your disability, as far as I can see, you haven't got one.'

'Perhaps I should tell the solicitor to call you to the stand as a character witness.' He gave a wintry smile. 'You can be certain that Sophie's parents will be trying to find people to support *their* case.'

'Why don't you tell him to call me, then? I'd be more than willing to testify,' she offered swiftly.

Cassie wondered briefly if her defence of Luke was revealing too much of her feeling towards him, but he seemed so despondent that he needed to know there was someone firmly in his corner.

'It doesn't matter how many people they find, Luke, they won't be able to change the fact that the Paynes are that much older than you,' she pointed out, hurriedly changing tack. 'How would they be able to cope with a young child, especially once she's fully mobile?'

'Don't forget, they're wealthy enough to be able to buy twenty-four-hour-a-day care while I'll have to depend on the hospital's crèche.' He shrugged almost fatalistically.

'I know coping by yourself won't be an ideal situation,' Cassie agreed, 'but it won't be that much different from many other single-parent families, and certainly not enough to warrant taking your child away.'

'Until they bring out their trump card,' he said hoarsely, his knuckles whitening as he wrapped his hands tightly around the mug. 'She's spent nearly half of her life so far living with them. I'm almost a stranger to her.'

'That's hardly your fault,' she objected heatedly. 'You weren't able to visit her because you were in hospital. Have you been seeing her regularly since you came out?'

'I've been round to their house on almost a daily basis but I've seen more of the two of them than I have of her. You'd be surprised how often I've been told she's asleep, or how quickly they can arrange for her to disappear out of the back door when I'm ringing the bell at the front.' He shook his head in frustration. 'And even when I *do* manage to see her, they don't leave the two of us alone.'

Cassie hadn't realised that the situation had already grown so tense. No wonder he'd been looking so strained since he'd returned to work.

'Is there some sort of supervision order?' she asked, half remembering the term from some television drama or other. 'If not, I don't think they can legally stop you from walking out of the house with her.'

'I can't do that to her,' he objected. 'She probably doesn't remember me very well, and the last thing I want to do is upset her. I was hoping that the two of them would agree to me building up the relationship by visiting for several days before I took her home. That would give me enough time to get myself ready to take on the full responsibility for her day-to-day care.'

Cassie dragged her eyes away from his despondent face and concentrated on putting down her mug of lukewarm coffee. What she really wanted to do was wrap him in her arms and promise him that everything would turn out all right, but she knew from her own experience that it wasn't always true.

'There's nothing to stop you getting the house straight, is there?' she pointed out. 'If it comes to a court case, they'll probably send some busybody social worker round to see if you keep your bathroom clean and pick up your dirty socks.'

He gave a startled chuckle. 'Trust you to bring things down to basics. Unfortunately, you're probably right about the social worker. You wouldn't consider volunteering to help a poor disabled man to get his house ready for inspection, would you?'

It was Cassie's turn to laugh and she threatened to pelt him with one of the throw pillows from the settee.

'Trust a man to find a way to get out of a rotten job!' she exclaimed while he pretended to cower. 'How bad is it? Will it need bulldozers or just a large shovel?'

She knew her objections were only token. If he needed her help she would be only too willing to give it to him, especially if it meant spending time in his company.

An insistent voice in the back of her head was reminding her that she wasn't going to let herself get dragged into a no-win situation but she did her best to ignore it. Unfortunately, the more time she spent with him the more involved she was likely to become.

Another idea suddenly came to her and before that insistent voice could intervene she heard herself speaking it aloud.

'If you want me to, I could come with you next time you go to see your daughter.'

She saw the startled expression on his face and hurried on. 'If I were to turn up on the doorstep with you as an old friend of Sophie's, wanting to reminisce with her parents and see her baby, perhaps the in-laws from hell would be less likely to shut the door in your face.'

Luke frowned, then his expression gradually lightened until it looked almost gleeful.

'You know, I think it might work!' he exclaimed. 'They're such sticklers for appearances that they wouldn't like their hospitality called into question. But are you sure you want to do that? It won't be the most comfortable of situations, especially with me in the room.'

'I'd love to go,' she assured him. 'It'll be my chance to strike a blow for justice. Anyway, we both know that once there's a baby in the room there'll be no shortage of conversation.'

In view of the imminent threat of legal sanctions, they decided that the attempt should be made early the following day.

'It'll give them less time to whisk her out of the way,' Luke pointed out.

'But that'll mean another morning without a lie-in,' Cassie groaned. 'And it's the only compensation I get for working a late shift.'

Luke suddenly looked stricken with remorse but, knowing that the situation concerning Jenny was more serious than her desire for a lazy morning, she hurried on, 'Of course, you could always make that state of affairs better by bringing me a special treat for breakfast when you come to pick me up.'

'Done!' His answering grin was a potent mixture of relief and fun. 'Anything in particular?'

'Surprise me.'

There was an extra spring in Cassie's step as she entered the unit later that morning and she was aware that a silly smile kept creeping across her face.

It didn't matter that she would be seeing Luke as usual when he came on duty—all she could think about was the new closeness that was developing between them.

'You're not going out together on a date,' she muttered when she caught sight of herself in the mirror over the basin. 'You know very well that you're just the means of Luke being with his daughter. Anyway, even if he was interested it's too soon. He's still missing Sophie.'

Something about the sound of her own voice in the confines of the staff washroom had the effect of bringing her feet firmly back to the ground.

Luke was just as much out of bounds now as he'd been once he'd made his choice and had married Sophie. Cassie had known then that there could never be an intimate relationship between them. She'd learned at first hand the heartache of being everybody's second choice and wasn't going to go through it again.

'*That's* where you've been hiding!' exclaimed a voice as she came out of the washroom a couple of minutes later, and she whirled to face her friend.

'Kirstin! What are you doing here?' Cassie took in the fact that a stethoscope bulged out of her friend's pocket and realised that she must be on duty, too.

'Just checking up on one of my babies,' she said, concern colouring her smile. 'How is Victoria Ford doing today?'

Cassie beckoned her into the department, her answering smile far more wholehearted.

'Come and see for yourself,' she invited, leading the way.

'Dr Whittaker. What are you doing here?' Cathy Ford asked with a guilty expression, her hand tightening convulsively on the edge of her baby's cot. 'You haven't come to tell me to go back to the ward, have you?'

'Not at all,' Kirstin soothed. 'I've actually come to see how our little girl is doing.'

'Great!' Tom Ford said with a beam. 'Come here and have a look at her. The doctor said she's doing so well that she won't have to stay in the special care unit much longer.'

'Hey! What's wrong with my unit? Don't you like the service we provide here?' Cassie teased.

'It's not that, Sister. Don't get me wrong—you've all been brilliant,' he said hastily. 'It's just that the sooner she doesn't need special care, the sooner she's well enough to come home with us.'

'We do know what you mean,' Kirstin said with a grin as she glanced up from her inspection of the tiny child. 'Just tell us that you're pleased with our handiwork. You know that her face is still very swollen after the operation. Everything will look different again once it settles down—'

'Oh, yes!' Cathy interrupted with a tearful smile. 'We know all that, but she *still* looks beautiful to us. More beautiful than we could have imagined. It's like a miracle to see her little face looking so different in just a few hours.'

'I always feel the same way,' Kirstin admitted conspiratorially. 'This part of the reconstruction was essential so that she can feed properly, but it was also necessary to safeguard her hearing. Before, the hole in the roof of her mouth would have made her prone to infections that could have left her deaf. When we see how well things have gone, we'll be able to decide about the timing for the rest of the reconstruction. 'We want to make sure that her mouth is all put right by the time she's starting to speak properly so that she won't have difficulty making herself understood.'

Cassie knew that the explanations would have been made several times before, but often parents were so worried about their precious babies that they didn't take everything in the first time or two. She hadn't a doubt that they would still be needing the same explanations when Victoria came in for the next episode of surgery.

'The scar will look red and angry when the dressing comes off,' Cassie reminded them, 'but it will gradually fade so that by the time Victoria's old enough to be interested in boys—'

'Don't!' Tom said with a dramatic shudder. 'I hate the thought of any hormone-crazed youth coming anywhere near my little girl. Once she reaches puberty I'm thinking of locking her in her room until she's at least thirty to keep her safe.'

'Go on,' his wife chided. 'It won't be that bad. Remember, you were that young once.'

'*That's* how I know what'll be going through their evil little minds and *that's* why I'm going to lock her safely away!' he exclaimed.

Cassie and Kirstin were still chuckling as they walked away.

'Is this one visit in a list of them, or have you got time for a coffee?' Cassie offered.

'Just a quick one,' Kirstin said after a glance at her watch. 'I've got one mum simmering and we don't know yet whether she's going to need a Caesarean, but I've got my bleeper with me.'

It didn't take long to boil the kettle. Cassie smiled when she realised that the two of them were already doing their usual—continuing a conversation as though it had been only a few minutes since they'd last spoken rather than days or even weeks.

'Naomi's dragging me out to visit Dot first thing tomorrow morning with the latest plans for the wedding,' Kirstin said cheerfully as she settled on the arm of a saggy old armchair and took her first sip of coffee. 'Will you be free to come with us? I think it's the short list of designs for the dresses we'll be wearing.'

'Of course I— Oh, no, I won't.' Cassie suddenly remembered just where she would be going tomorrow morning and was startled to feel a creeping tide of heat flood up her throat and over her face.

'Aha!' Kirstin pounced gleefully. 'And where will you be...or, more to the point, with whom?'

For several long seconds Cassie was completely tongue-tied as thoughts and emotions vied for attention. If she told Kirstin who she was going to be with, her friend was going to make assumptions, and she wasn't at liberty to tell her *why* she and Luke were actually going to be together. The fact that one small part of her was still longing for their outing to be a bona fide date was something she didn't want to contemplate.

'I'm going with Luke—' she began but didn't get any further.

'Luke! But I thought you'd decided he was permanently off your list. When did you change your mind?'

It wasn't the first time Cassie had regretted the way the three of them tended to spill out their deepest thoughts and feelings. It also didn't help that Kirstin seemed to remember every one of them verbatim.

'He's still off my list,' she declared hastily. 'There's nothing personal in it. I'm just helping him out with something tomorrow morning.'

'Hmm.' Kirstin looked sceptical but there must have been something on Cassie's face that deterred her from pursuing the topic.

Grateful for her friend's tact, Cassie hastily changed the direction of the conversation.

Later, Cassie found herself hovering in front of her wardrobe, trying to decide what to wear the next day.

There was already a pile of discarded clothes on the end of her bed and a quick glance at her bedside clock told her that if she didn't make a decision soon, it would be time to get up before she went to bed.

With a pair of smart summer-weight trousers in one hand and an understated cotton dress in the other she caught sight of herself in the mirror and stopped in her tracks.

'What on earth am I doing?' she demanded aloud as she thrust both garments back on the rail. 'It's not some fashion parade I'll be taking part in. I'm only going with Luke to give him a chance to spend some time with his daughter.'

With speed born of anger she swiftly restored the jumble of discarded clothes to their rightful places and dragged out her faithful jeans.

'It's not a date,' she muttered fiercely as she hung them up on the back of her bedroom door with a plain cotton shirt. 'Just keep that fact in your head, my girl. It's not a date and it will never be a date because, as far as you're concerned, Luke Thornton is out of bounds.'

CHAPTER FOUR

'COME on, Cassie! Hurry up and open the door!' said an impatient voice when she answered the intercom the following morning.

She blinked in surprise and silently pressed the button to activate the release of the front door. Luke definitely sounded a bit…stressed this morning, she thought as she went to open her front door. Not at all his usual polite self.

Perhaps he'd come to tell her that he'd thought better of their plan and didn't need her to come with him. Her heart sank like a lead weight. She'd really been looking forward to spending a few hours in his company, even though it would only be as a friend. And even if he *had* been ready to start dating again, he wouldn't choose her. Well, he hadn't the first time round, had he? And she hadn't changed in the meantime.

At the sound of footsteps she pulled the door wide and Luke appeared with a pile of boxes and bags stacked right up under his chin.

'Cassie. Thank God. Grab something quickly before I drop the lot,' he begged in the same strained voice she'd heard over the intercom, and she couldn't help laughing aloud.

'What on earth is all this?' she demanded as she relieved him of half of the load. 'And how on earth did you press the intercom button with both hands full?'

'You don't want to know,' he warned darkly. 'It wasn't a pretty sight.'

'The mind boggles,' she said with a chuckle as she led the way into her tiny kitchen. 'What do you want me to do with these? Do you want me to get some plates out or—'

'If you just put them on the end of the work surface, I'll take care of everything,' he announced grandly as he deposited his own burden. He grabbed a towel and tucked it in the top of a pair of faded jeans which were almost the twin of hers and rubbed his hands together like a concert pianist preparing for a recital. 'If you like you can go and put your feet up while you're waiting to eat.'

'It's only fair that I should at least set the table. Anyway, I'd rather watch what you're doing,' she countered, not quite trusting the idea of Luke set loose in her kitchen. After all, she'd seen how untidy his own kitchen cupboards were just the other day.

'Aha! You prefer to see the maestro at work!' he quipped gleefully. 'Prepare to be amazed by his skill and dexterity in all things culinary.'

With a flourish he opened a polystyrene carton of eggs and promptly dropped one.

His expression of dismay was so comical that Cassie couldn't help laughing.

'Perhaps the maestro could do with a minion to come round after him and clear up?' she suggested through her chuckles as she put down the cutlery and reached for a handful of disposable towel instead.

'Perhaps,' he conceded loftily, then lost his control and laughed aloud. 'But I'm not usually so clumsy.'

'I know you're not, or I wouldn't let you near my patients,' Cassie pointed out as she disposed of the remains. 'They'd probably shatter just as easily as this egg did if you dropped them, and they aren't nearly as easy to replace.'

'I'm glad they don't come in half-dozens and dozens either. Can you imagine how we'd have to have the incubators redesigned? Racks of identical egg-babies in each one.'

While Luke continued unpacking a selection of intriguing packages and Cassie set the table in her sitting room, the light-hearted conversation meandered onto an article Cassie had read about a parenting project in a local school.

'The children were divided into pairs and made responsible for the care of an egg for a week. They had to treat it as if it were a newborn baby,' she explained as she watched him deftly prepare two grapefruit halves, before assembling ingredients in one of her jugs and helping himself to a whisk. 'They had to keep a diary of routine things such as feeding times and nappy changes, and they couldn't go out anywhere without one of them being responsible for taking care of the egg.'

'That's OK as far as it goes,' Luke interrupted, 'but it doesn't let them know what it's like when a baby has you up night after night until you're so tired you don't know how to put one foot in front of the other without falling over.'

'They thought of that, too, by enlisting the parents' help to set alarm clocks to go off in the night.'

'Clever.' Luke chuckled. 'Did the report say what the children thought of the scheme?'

'That was the best part, as far as I was concerned,' said Cassie with relish. 'The project was triggered because the school had an increasing number of under-age pupils getting pregnant. They were interviewed about their attitudes towards teenage pregnancies before the scheme started and then again at the end to see if there was any change.'

'And?' He glanced up from the perfect circle of pancake batter he was pouring into her best frying pan.

'Before, quite a few of them were really starry-eyed about the idea of having a perfect cuddly baby of their own. Most of them seemed to regard it as a slightly more sophisticated version of their favourite doll.

Afterwards, there was only one of the girls who was still interested in starting a family in the near future. The rest of them had all decided that the minute-by-minute responsibilities were far more than they wanted to take on. Some had even decided that they might never bother to have children at all if they were that much of a tie.'

'That's all well and good as far as it went, but was it really fair to show them only the negative side of parenthood that way?' Luke commented as he peered under the grill and prodded at something. 'What about all the special things like cuddles and smiles and first steps?'

'That side is only too well covered by advertisers trying to sell baby food and disposable nappies,' Cassie countered. 'It's the part that you *never* see in the adverts that comes as a shock.'

'You mean, the fact that their volume can rival Concorde on take-off when they really start shouting? And the fact that their nappies don't stay sweet and clean for more than a nanosecond?'

'And the fact that a small bottle of milk can cover an area twice the size of a football field when they bring it back up? Yes. That sort of thing,' she agreed wryly.

'Well, they won't have learned any of that from looking after an egg, but if it's made a few of them decide to wait a year or two more before they risk pregnancy I'm all for it,' he said, straightening up and wiping his hands on the towel wrapped around his waist. 'Right, madame,

I believe your breakfast is ready. If you would like to seat yourself.'

'It certainly smells wonderful. What's on the menu?'

Cassie allowed him to seat her ceremonially at her little table. He whisked the towel away from his waist and draped it over his arm to bow at her like an obsequious waiter.

'Your starter is a sun-ripened grapefruit lovingly prepared and served *au naturel.*' He frowned when she gave a giggle. 'Oops! That didn't come out quite right, did it? It's the grapefruit that's served *au naturel*, not the waiter.'

'Pity,' Cassie murmured softly with an assessing glance from the top of his gleaming brown hair to his trainers-clad feet.

'Madame! I'm *not* that sort of man!' he exclaimed in mock horror, his hands spread theatrically across the front of his deep blue shirt right over his heart.

'Pity,' she repeated, suddenly discovering how much fun this sort of teasing could be. She'd never had time for it while she'd been concentrating on her career, and over the last couple of years she hadn't been particularly interested in sparring with any of the other potential suitors who'd entered her orbit. Once she'd met Luke they'd all seemed to pale into insignificance, even after he'd married and taken himself out of her reach for ever.

She was chuckling when her eyes met his but when she saw the strangely intent expression in their blue depths she grew still, suddenly feeling like vulnerable prey which had realised it has been spotted by a dangerous predator.

'Luke?' she murmured uncertainly, unable to draw breath in the seemingly airless tension between them. Her heart thumped unevenly when his gaze dropped briefly to her mouth, then his lashes swept swiftly down and, as if they had wiped all trace of the expression with their passage, it was gone.

'As I was saying…' He paused to clear his throat, but his voice was still slightly husky when he continued. 'If you'd like to start with your grapefruit, the next course will be ready shortly.'

Cassie was glad to have something to focus on but she hoped that Luke wasn't watching her because there was a visible tremor in the spoon when she scooped out the first segment of grapefruit.

She was uncomfortably silent until he brought her a plate of perfectly fluffy scrambled eggs with golden brown triangles of toast.

'Scrambled eggs. How did you know that's my favourite way of eating them? These look absolutely perfect,' she exclaimed as she reached for her cutlery.

'You're lucky you like them the same way I do, then. I can't bear them all solid and rubbery, or all runny and sloppy.'

The silence was less fraught then, and when he left for the kitchen with the announcement that he was going to bring in his pièce de résistance they were almost back on their old footing.

'Time for a drum roll,' he declared as he carried two plates in at shoulder height, one on each hand.

'Oh, wow! That looks so good,' Cassie exclaimed when she saw the crêpes filled with fresh strawberries and whipped cream. 'I never realised that you were such an accomplished cook.'

'I'd like to bask in your admiration but, I have to admit, you've sampled almost my whole repertoire in one meal. I'll save the grilled steak or the baked beans on toast options for another time.'

Another time. Cassie's heart gave a silly hop at the idea

that Luke might actually want to spend time with her, but she quickly subdued it with a hefty dose of logic.

How many times did people make conversation by saying 'we'll have to do this again', without meaning a word of it? The only reason he was here now was because he desperately wanted to spend time with his daughter. There was no point in pinning her hopes on any other meals like this.

'Well, all I can say is that you certainly lived up to your part of the bargain,' she said, looking up at him just long enough to flash him a bright smile. 'This is certainly ample compensation for missing out on a lie-in. I only hope the rest of the morning is as successful.'

'Ready?' Luke asked as he released his seat belt.

Cassie looked back at him, dragging her eyes away from the impressive front door they would shortly approach. If anything, he looked even less keen to take the next step than she did.

'Are you?' she countered, her compassion such that she dared to reach out one hand to rest it over the white knuckles gripping the steering-wheel. 'We don't have to do this if you'd rather not.'

He closed his eyes for a moment and Cassie noticed anew how tired he was looking. No wonder, if he had this situation preying on his mind all the time. She didn't think she'd have been able to sleep much either.

'If I don't, I won't stand a chance of spending time with Jenny, and you can just guess how Sophie's parents will construe that when it comes to a court case.'

'You mean, ''Your honour, he's never once spent any time with his daughter since he came out of hospital'' sort of thing?'

'And without ever mentioning the fact that the reason

I didn't see her was because they made it impossible? Yes, that's exactly what I'm afraid of.'

'In that case, what are we waiting for?' Cassie demanded as she reached for the doorhandle. 'Let's go and shoot that ploy right out of the water.'

Luke had joined her by the time she'd crossed the immaculate gravel driveway and they climbed the steps side by side.

When Cassie saw the expression that crossed the older woman's face when she opened the door and saw Luke standing there she realised that, if anything, he had downplayed the animosity towards him.

For a moment it looked as if, in spite of the presence of another person, the door was going to be closed in his face again, and Cassie couldn't allow that to happen.

'Mrs Payne,' she said brightly, stepping forward with her hand outstretched. 'I know it's very rude and I hope you won't mind me dropping by, unannounced, but it's so long since I've seen your granddaughter, and when Luke said he was coming to visit I couldn't resist the opportunity.'

Cassie knew that her babbling made her sound like an empty-headed idiot but it was having the desired effect. They were inside the house—at least, as far as the hallway.

'Obviously, we didn't know what her routine was, and we realise that she might still be asleep at the moment,' she continued, edging her way across the hallway towards the first open door in the hope that it was a sitting room of some sort. 'But I'm hoping that you might have a few photographs I could look at while we're waiting. Has she grown very much? Is her hair still as blonde and curly as Sophie's?'

By the time she ran out of things to say she'd also run

out of breath and sank gratefully into the plush embrace of an ivory-coloured settee.

'Yes, she's grown and her hair... Excuse me, but do I know you?' Mrs Payne's confusion finally overcame her formal manners. 'Are you...? *Were* you a friend of Sophie's?'

'Oh, how silly of me,' Cassie said with a wide smile. 'You had so much on your mind when we were finally introduced that you couldn't possibly remember, but Sophie must have mentioned me often in connection with work. I'm Cassie Mills.'

Out of sight of the chilly grey eyes she had her fingers tightly crossed, but she didn't breathe a sigh of relief until she saw the socially correct smile lift just the corners of Mrs Payne's mouth.

'Oh, Cassie. Of course,' she murmured, but Cassie was almost certain from the slightly baffled expression on the woman's face that she hadn't been remembered at all.

It was hardly likely. After all, their first brief introduction had taken all of five seconds in the reception line at Luke's and Sophie's wedding, and they hadn't come face to face at all at Jenny's christening.

Still, it was imperative for Luke's sake that she take advantage of the leeway she'd just gained.

'Did you say you had some photos?' she asked, her eagerness unfeigned. 'I work with the very tiny babies at St Augustine's and you might think that I'd have enough of them at work but I adore them.'

The photo album was leather-bound and Cassie thought it looked almost as if it had been professionally assembled rather than lovingly collected by doting grandparents.

Still, having manoeuvred the older woman into sitting between Luke and herself on the settee, she wasn't about to find fault.

The first page made her very uncomfortable, with its juxtaposed images of baby Jenny and her dead mother at exactly the same age. Unfortunately, each page was the same, the child's development charted exactly against her mother's progress a quarter of a century earlier.

In the photos taken over the last few months even the child's clothing appeared eerily identical, almost as if the Paynes were trying to recreate history.

It was enough to raise the hairs on the back of Cassie's neck.

'Is she really as pretty as her pictures?' she challenged, hoping to direct the course of the conversation in a way that would put them in the same room as Jenny.

Would the obviously indulgent grandmother take it up? So far they hadn't heard a single sound to show that a young child lived in the house.

'Of course she is,' Mrs Payne retorted instantly, and snapped the book shut. 'Come and see for yourself.'

She rose regally from her position between them, apparently unhampered by her narrow skirt and slender heels, and led the way, the photo album cradled against her chest as though it was too precious to put down.

'How did you do that?' Luke murmured softly as they followed her along the hallway, their footsteps almost totally silent in the thick pile carpet.

Cassie had noticed that he'd barely said a word since they'd arrived at the front door, apparently content to confine himself to approving sounds as he'd viewed his little daughter's recent life in a series of frozen poses.

'Feminine wiles,' she whispered back, careful that her voice didn't carry to the woman in front of them.

They were right outside the door at the top of the house before they heard the sound of a baby whimpering.

'That's enough of that,' said a stern voice as the door

swung open to reveal a tall, elderly woman in a formal uniform. 'We don't like little girls to make nasty noises like that, do we?'

'Ah, Nanny. I've brought you some visitors, if it's convenient,' Mrs Payne announced as she swept in.

'Well, madam, I was just about to give Jennifer Ann her morning bath, as you can see.' She gestured to the baby who was lying on a changing mat clothed only in a traditional cloth nappy.

'Jennywren...'

Cassie heard Luke's hoarse whisper and was certain he was just about to lose his steely control. If he were to stride across the room now to grab his daughter, all hell would probably break loose.

She surreptitiously grabbed hold of his arm to restrain him and could feel the tremors in his taut muscles.

'Oh, what a little angel!' she trilled, horribly aware that every eye was now riveted on her as she released her hold on him and hurried into the room. She almost had to barge Mrs Payne out of the way. 'Oh, please, do let me bath her. I promise I won't drop her. After all, I've had plenty of practice.'

She swooped down on the wide-eyed infant, forcing the stiffly uniformed nanny to take a rapid step to get out of her way, then paused deliberately.

'Hello, precious,' she crooned softly, reverting to her normal voice so that she didn't frighten Luke's little daughter. 'How would you like me to give you your bath today?'

The silent pause almost made it seem as though the little mite was considering the question, but just seconds later she gave a beaming smile and held her arms up.

'Well, now. That looked like a yes,' Cassie announced to her fascinated audience as she scooped her up and cradled her against a shoulder. 'Come on, Daddy. It's bath-time,' she prompted, and whirled towards the open bathroom door.

'I'm still wet through,' Luke grumbled an hour and a half later as he guided his car out of the imposing gates.

'But was it worth it?' Cassie hardly needed to ask. Just one look at Luke's face as he'd wrapped his precious daughter in an enormous dry towel and cradled her in his arms had been enough.

'You know it was. I'd still be there with her if we didn't have to get you back to go to work.' His face was wreathed in the first real smile she'd seen since he'd returned to work after the accident. 'Ah, Cassie, I don't know how I'll ever be able to thank you. And as for that fancy footwork with the cast-iron nanny...'

Cassie chuckled. 'She certainly had plenty of starch in her uniform. I began to wonder if she would crack if she bent over.'

'Well, she was certainly well softened up by the time you'd finished. To have her persuade the mother-in-law from hell that it was a good idea for Jenny to spend the weekend with me was a stroke of genius.'

'Well, it would hardly do the Paynes' credibility much good if the nanny could confirm in court that they'd prevented you from spending time with your daughter,' Cassie pointed out, unwilling to take too much credit. 'Anyway, I doubt that she'd have taken the idea up if she didn't like you. In spite of her starchiness and the fact that she's a bit abrupt and old-fashioned, I think she's really fond of Jenny.'

'Hmm,' he said doubtfully, obviously remembering the stern expression on the older woman's face when they'd first seen her.

'How could she *not* fall in love with her? She's a beautiful child,' Cassie declared fervently. 'With those big blue eyes and blonde curls she looks like a little angel. The Paynes have certainly spared no expense in taking care of her while you've been in hospital.' The nursery suite had been fairly simply decorated, but everything was obviously very expensive.

'I'll admit that I don't know what I'd have done without their help, but...' He sighed.

'But it's time for Jenny to come home now,' she finished for him.

'Yes. And I owe you a huge debt for getting them to agree so easily to letting her visit this weekend.'

'You shouldn't have said that,' she warned, trying to lighten the conversation by teasing. 'It was a very dangerous admission, especially after that wonderful breakfast this morning. Now I shall have to think of some way you can repay me.'

'Good morning, Sister,' Luke said formally when they met on the ward the next day. 'Isn't it a lovely day?'

Cassie glanced briefly out of the nearby window at the unexpectedly dismal turn the weather had taken and raised her eyebrows. They'd had a spell of fine weather over the last couple of weeks, a real flaming June, but the bright sunshine which had accompanied them on their journey yesterday had disappeared behind hazy mist today.

'Beautiful!' she agreed with irony heavy in her tone. She hadn't seen him since he'd insisted on dropping her off at St Augustine's yesterday afternoon. 'I'm glad I know what's made you so cheerful or I'd be wondering if you were in your right mind.'

He grinned. 'Isn't it amazing what a good night's sleep

will do? I don't think I moved a muscle until the alarm went off.'

He certainly looked better, his expression alert and his eyes gleaming brightly with good humour.

Cassie was glad to see the change in him. This was far more like it. This was the Luke she knew and— Her mind veered sharply away from completing the thought. 'Knew and loved' was only an expression that people used, that was all.

'So you spent yesterday evening getting everything ready for Jenny's visit and now you're ready to tackle a full shift?'

'Well, it's getting there,' he temporised as Cassie led the way into the little office. One of her hands went to switch on the kettle while the other reached out to activate the computer screen to bring up the latest observations on each of their little charges.

'I hadn't realised just how much stuff I'd accumulated over the last few years until I started to unpack it,' he continued to murmur as he scanned the information on the screen. 'I had the removal firm clear the house out while I was still in hospital and I've found some very strange things in the bottom of boxes.'

'Strange things?'

'Yes.' He glanced up at her with a grin. 'Like the carefully wrapped jar of marmalade with just one spoonful left in the bottom and the remains of a packet of soggy chocolate biscuits. And the contents of my laundry basket—unwashed,' he added with a grimace.

Cassie chuckled at his disgusted expression. 'If you think about it, they probably have to be very careful to pack everything. They could throw something away thinking it's worthless junk, and discover it was a priceless work of art bought from one of these modern exhibitions.'

Something on the screen had caught his full attention and that was the end of the banter.

'Neesha is still getting episodes of bradycardia,' he muttered as he scanned the observations taken since he'd last been on duty.

'But at least she seems to be remembering to breathe these days,' Cassie pointed out. 'And she's putting on a bit of weight.'

'Minimal,' Luke dismissed with a scowl. 'Are you sure a gnat didn't land on the scales while you were weighing her?'

'Certainly not! And even a tiny gain is still better than losing weight,' she insisted. 'That little girl is going to be all right. You just wait and see.'

She tilted her chin up at him and surprised a strange expression in his eyes.

'You really care, don't you?' he said quietly, just when she was beginning to feel a little uncomfortable under the intensity of his regard. 'They're not even your children but you care as much as if they were.'

'So do you,' she pointed out a little defensively. 'Or do you think I've never caught you coming back into the unit for one last look before you go off duty?'

'Guilty as charged,' he admitted rather sheepishly. 'A good pair, aren't we? Probably both too conscientious for our own good.'

'Or we're both mad,' she countered. 'That's probably why we chose this field of medicine.' Her words emerged sounding quite ordinary and she saw him smile at the implied insult, but all she could hear echoing around inside her head as he left the room was his throw-away remark. 'A good pair, aren't we?' he'd said, and he would never know how much she wished that could have been true.

CHAPTER FIVE

'LUKE? You're wanted on the phone,' Cassie called as he was about to leave the department late on Friday afternoon.

'Who is it?' He paused with one foot each side of the doorway threshold as though loath to stop.

The impression was true, Cassie knew, even though it was unusual to see him so keen to leave. But, then, tonight was his last chance to get Jenny's room ready for her to come home for her weekend's visit tomorrow.

'He wouldn't say. Just that it was important to talk to you in person.'

The smile he'd been wearing all day slipped into a scowl as he reversed direction and made for the office.

'Thornton,' he announced succinctly as he propped one hip on the corner of the desk.

Within seconds the scowl had metamorphosed into an expression of pure anger and he was on his feet, every muscle tensed with the explosive need to hit something.

'Surely they can't do that?' he demanded harshly. 'I'm her father, for God's sake. Don't I have *any* rights?'

Cassie's heart sank. Even though she was doing her best not to eavesdrop, she could guess only too easily what the phone call was about.

It wasn't long before the receiver was slammed down to the accompaniment of a ripe curse.

'Luke...' Cassie hurried towards the open door of the office and swung it closed, a silent reminder to him that relatives of their little patients could overhear what he was saying—especially when he was too angry to remember to lower his voice.

'Sorry!' he apologised, and raked the fingers of both hands through his hair, grabbing hold of fistfuls as though contemplating yanking it out by the roots.

'That was my solicitor on the phone with a message from the Paynes' solicitor. Do you know what they've done?' he demanded, his anger somehow even more potent when voiced in a harsh semi-whisper. 'Do you know what that self-centred pair have done?'

'I can guess. Put off the day Jenny can visit at short notice to one when you're on duty?'

'Worse than that,' he growled. 'They've decided, on the advice of their solicitor, that until my home and I have undergone a full inspection as to our suitability for a visit, Jennywren won't be allowed to come home with me at all.'

The Paynes' selfishness almost took Cassie's breath away. How could they be so cruel to Luke? Not only must he be feeling Sophie's loss just as badly as they were, but he was also still recovering from his own injuries.

Realising that voicing her thoughts would only stoke the heat of his anger, she opted for a more positive topic.

'So, who do you have to contact and how long will it take to get this official inspection organised?'

'I haven't got a clue,' he admitted, flinging both hands in the air. 'If it's just a delaying tactic they're probably hoping that it will take at least eighteen years.'

'Did you ask your solicitor?' she prompted, knowing full well that he hadn't.

'I was too angry with the Paynes to think about it,' he admitted. 'I was just so…so shocked that they would go back on their word like that.' He glanced at his watch and cursed again. 'The solicitor was just about to leave his office and it's too late now to get hold of someone else for advice.'

'Not necessarily.' Cassie reached for the computer keyboard and tapped a series of buttons to search through the hospital's information database, then picked up the phone and began to dial.

'Who are you ringing? You haven't got a tame lawyer on hand, hidden in the basement?'

'Better than that,' she quipped with a triumphant grin as the call was answered. She held the receiver out to him. 'The hospital retains legal representation, remember. They're probably more used to dealing with contract law and malpractice suits but we sometimes get stuck in the middle of custody battles so they should be able to tell you the basics of what you need to know.'

Although she would dearly have liked to have stayed to listen to his half of the conversation, there were limits to her nosiness and she quickly left the room.

She desperately wanted to know how the conversation in the office was going, and if she was going to survive, without pressing her ear against the door to find out, she was going to have to keep herself busy.

If Luke wanted her to know what he'd found out he would tell her. She only hoped that he made the decision before she died of unsatisfied curiosity.

'Sister,' a voice called softly from the entrance of the ward, and she saw Tom Ford beckoning her over.

In the last couple of days there had been some changes in both the patients and the staff in the department, and one had been Tom's daughter, Victoria, who no longer needed special care.

'What can I do for you?' Cassie asked when she joined him outside the door. 'There aren't any problems with Victoria, are there?'

'No. Not at all,' he hastened to reassure her. 'As you know, she recovered so quickly after her cleft palate operation that she was moved fairly quickly out of special care into the paediatric ward.'

'Yes. It was quite amazing how quickly the post-operative swelling went down, wasn't it? How is she doing now? What did the surgeon say when he saw her today?'

'She's doing fantastically well,' he said enthusiastically. 'She's already graduated from tube-feeding to suckling properly for the first time and the surgeon promised that, providing she doesn't have any infection, as soon as her stitches are removed we'll be able to take her home.'

'I'm so pleased for you.' She reached out to squeeze his arm, delighted with his good news. 'Thank you very much for coming across and giving me a progress report. I'll be sure to pass the news on to the rest of the staff.'

'Cathy and I just wanted to thank all of you for looking after us while Victoria was in your care,' he said, his cheeks flushed with embarrassment. 'While we were sitting beside her, we overheard some of the teasing that went on between the doctors and nurses over who keeps pinching all the chocolate biscuits so we wondered...would you accept these from us and share them between all of you?'

He proffered the carrier bag which Cassie hadn't even noticed in his other hand and she peered inside.

'Oh, wow! "A luxury selection of chocolate biscuits",' she read from the side of the tin. 'Are you sure I can't just make these disappear into the drawer of my desk and keep them for myself?'

'Do you honestly think I wouldn't be able to smell them?' demanded a voice behind her, as Luke joined them in the corridor with a broad smile on his face. 'Especially when they're my favourites.'

'*All* chocolate biscuits are your favourites,' Cassie retorted swiftly. 'And if the rest of us are going to get a look-in while you're around, I'm going to have to put these under lock and key.'

Tom burst out laughing at Luke's pout.

'That's one of the things that made our daughter's time in the unit bearable,' he said through his chuckles. 'You can be dealing with life-and-death situations minute by minute in there, but you still find the resilience to smile and tease each other. I take my hat off to the lot of you, because I certainly couldn't do it.'

He tipped an imaginary hat in salute and made his farewells. 'Don't fight over the biscuits,' he called back as he pushed open the door at the other end of the unit.

Cassie gave a wave then turned to face Luke, hoping that he might have come to tell her about his phone call.

It only took one glance at his face, now that the smile had faded, to tell that it hadn't been good news.

'Luke?' she prompted gently.

'Not good,' he answered succinctly, knowing what she was asking. 'The upshot of the conversation is that I've got to scrub and tidy my house in preparation for some Nosy Parker to decide whether I'm allowed to have a visit—just a visit, mind you—from my own daughter.'

'Oh, Luke,' she murmured. He looked so devastated that she wanted to wrap her arms round him to comfort him, but that wasn't possible. They just didn't have that sort of relationship, but that didn't mean she couldn't offer another sort of assistance. 'When are you going to start the marathon?'

'Marathon?' he frowned, obviously not following.

'The herculean task of sorting your house out,' she explained. 'Could you do with an extra pair of hands? After all, the sooner it's done, the sooner you can have Jenny to yourself.'

'You don't have to do that. It's not your problem,' he objected.

'I know it isn't, but I'm still offering. That's what friends are for,' she reminded him gently.

He was silent for a long moment, his blue eyes fixed very intently on her face before the corners of his mouth lifted into a ghost of a smile.

'In that case, friend, I'd be very grateful for the help. I've been out of hospital long enough that I should have the whole place straight by now, but somehow I just haven't had the heart,' he admitted, then took out his diary to compare their duties over the next few days.

They'd barely made the arrangement that he'd collect her after work the next day when his pager shrilled at him and he reached for the phone.

'Thornton. Special Care Baby Unit,' he said. There was a pause. 'When?' he asked, and added after a pause, 'Damn. I'm on my way.'

'Problem?' Cassie's adrenaline was already racing around her body in response to the tension in his voice.

'The Chen twins. They haven't been able to stop Lisa's labour and one baby is in distress. They're having to do an emergency Caesarean, starting in a matter of minutes.'

'Damn,' Cassie muttered, echoing Luke's response. The unit had been warned about the twins almost as soon as their presence had been detected at the mother's eight-week scan, but they certainly hadn't been expecting them to arrive this soon. 'How many weeks are they?'

'Thirty, plus four days,' he said with a grimace. 'If it was a single pregnancy I wouldn't be worried, and even an ordinary set of twins would have a damn good chance at this stage, but when they're conjoined...'

He didn't need to say any more. Cassie had joined the unit in time to see another set of Siamese twins undergoing intensive care in an attempt at saving their lives. Unfortunately, the weaker twin's badly malformed heart hadn't survived the first day, and the emergency operation to separate the live twin had barely started when he'd succumbed, too.

'We'll be ready and waiting,' she confirmed, suddenly desperate that these babies shouldn't suffer the same fate. Some people might have regarded them as nature's nightmares but she'd always looked on all the different sorts of twins as nature's special miracles.

Her thoughts continued as she hurried to make certain that everything would be ready for the twins' arrival, enlisting Staff Nurse Sahru Ismail to assist.

'Have you ever seen Siamese twins before?' she asked the young Sudanese woman, struck anew by the beauty of her dark butterscotch-coloured skin and flawless profile. She hadn't been working in the unit very long, having only recently moved to St Augustine's Hospital from one of its London counterparts.

'I have only seen them on a film when I was training,' Sahru answered. 'Do we know how much these twins are joined?'

'From the scans, it looks as if their skeletons are completely separate, but we know already that they share some organs. This is partly why they must be born quickly as one baby is starving the other.'

While they were speaking she was preparing two sets of monitoring equipment as each baby would have to be connected up separately.

'As the babies are arriving in duplicate, so must the

equipment be,' Sahru commented in her slightly stilted English. 'Is it time for the incubator to wait upstairs?'

The theatre was on the floor above them and, assuming they survived the trauma of their birth, the babies would be placed into the prepared incubator ready to travel down to the unit. Who knew exactly how many hours, days and weeks it would remain their home until they were ready for life out in the big wide world?

Once the staff were in position outside the operating theatre, they didn't have long to wait before they heard the sound of a single querulous cry. Cassie held her breath while she waited for another cry and found herself standing with her fingers tightly crossed.

She and Sahru had both tried but they'd discovered there was no point in looking through the windows inset into the theatre doors because there were so many people grouped around the table that it was impossible to see anything. As with any birth, there was a separate team of staff for each of the patients which, in this case, meant three complete teams grouped around a single table.

There was another cry and Sahru turned to her with an excited look on her face.

'That was a different voice. They are both alive,' she declared with a wide, delighted smile.

'So far,' Cassie cautioned, her gaze caught by the sight of Luke's familiar broad shoulders as he bent over in concentration.

She didn't need to be able to see him working to know how gentle he was being, his long-fingered hands infinitely tender as he checked his patient over to make sure she was stable enough to make the journey down to the unit.

She was still looking at him when he finally straightened up with a single carefully swaddled bundle in his arms and approached the new mother. Cassie watched his face carefully as he introduced mother and babies and released a small sigh of relief when she couldn't pick up any sign of tension in him. There was just a beaming smile that told her he was congratulating both parents on the birth of their little children.

After they'd had a brief chance to say hello it was time for Special Care to take over.

'We need to go via the ultrasound room,' Luke directed as they set off towards the bank of lifts.

Cassie permitted herself a small smile of relief. The tiny duo were already in a heated, oxygen-rich environment and Luke obviously wasn't in a desperate rush to get them to the unit if he was happy to do a quick detour for an ultrasound scan. That definitely seemed hopeful.

She found herself holding her breath when she helped to unwrap the little girls' bodies to allow the probe to pass over their naked skin, wondering exactly what she was about to see.

'They look so strange,' whispered Sahru in a hushed voice, her expression half intrigued, half horrified. 'It is almost as if they have melted together inside the mother.'

'That's exactly what it looks like,' Luke agreed with a small smile. 'It's strange to think that the cause is almost exactly the opposite.'

'Why does this happen?' Sahru asked as Luke spread conductive jelly over the delicate skin of their joined stomachs and positioned the high-tech probe ready to begin the first scan. 'I have been taught about nursing such as these but why did they not just become two in the normal way of twins?'

'Purely because of the timing of the division,' Luke explained, his tone slightly preoccupied as he split his attention between the positioning of the probe and the images forming on the screen. 'If the bundle of cells had divided one week after fertilisation, they would have just been a set of identical twins. If it happened one and a half weeks after, they would be ''mirror'' twins, one of them right-handed and the other left-, but if the division happens at two weeks or later the babies will be Siamese twins with the degree of connection being more and more the longer it takes.'

'How badly conjoined are they?' Cassie asked, her eyes flicking from the images on the screen to the intent expression on Luke's face. She knew he could see something he didn't like when she saw him frowning, and wondered how serious it was.

He pressed some keys on the computer keyboard to copy the images as a permanent record for future reference, then left one image frozen on the monitor.

'It's a little difficult to see on this two-dimensional representation, but their skeletons have formed completely separately. They have one healthy kidney each, here and here, and share a third deformed one between them.' He outlined the various structures with the tip of one finger as he spoke and Sahru nodded as the shadowy images began to make sense.

'That's not a perfect situation, but at least they have one healthy one each,' Luke continued, frowning as he concentrated on the scan. 'No. *This* is where the major problem is. Their livers are joined so that twin one has a lobe twice the size of twin two's, hence the blood supply is similarly unbalanced. This means that twin two isn't getting a fair share of nutrient-rich blood. Also, now that they've been born and their mother is no longer doing it for them, their liver has to take on the extra task of cleaning their blood.'

'So the second baby was being starved by the first one

even before they were born?' Sahru questioned as she helped to guide the incubator towards their unit.

'In effect, yes. The situation was being closely monitored as the pregnancy progressed because we were hoping to delay the birth as long as twin two wasn't in any danger. Unfortunately, the mother's body took the decision out of our hands when she went into labour and we couldn't stop it.'

'What will happen to them now?' Sahru asked, voicing Cassie's thoughts.

'That will depend on how quickly we can stabilise the two of them and whether we can give twin two enough extra support to make up for the unequal blood supply. Ultimately, they'll need to be separated, and the preliminary scans show that it should be a fairly straightforward job. But even though they've got the added advantage of being girls, we'd still rather not do it while they're this premature unless it's a life-or-death emergency. Ideally, they need to be much bigger and stronger before they can safely go through such trauma, and the actual mechanics of the operation means that we need several weeks for preparation if it's to be a success. It would take that long to use tissue expanders to grow enough skin around the area to cover both wounds after separation.'

The incubator was wheeled into position and the task began to connect each twin to a separate bank of monitoring equipment.

They were quickly surrounded by an array of sleek high-tech stands and a bewildering number of boxes, buttons and monitors with multicoloured readouts of every description.

'I take it you two will be taking care of these two?' Luke queried as he checked everything one last time and settled the clear plastic cover over the twins, like some strange tent covering two almost naked baby birds in a nest composed of coils of thin plastic tubing.

'For this shift, yes,' Cassie confirmed, and reached for the camera she'd set out ready. 'Have you any idea how long it will be before the parents can come and visit? I know their mum and dad saw them before you had to take them away, but it's not the same as taking their time to have a really good look. Anyway, I expect they'd like to have a photo to show the rest of the family.'

She set the camera controls for taking a close-up shot and moved a little closer to the twins, careful to focus the shot on their tiny perfect faces.

'Mum can come down as soon as Sam Dysart says she's recovered enough from the operation, but I expect their dad will arrive fairly soon.' Luke accepted the rapidly developing photo and smiled at the result. 'Perfect shot. It looks almost as if it's one baby looking into a mirror at an exact reflection.'

'Excuse me,' said a hesitant voice from the doorway, and all three of them looked across at the slightly distracted man hovering there in a rumpled blue gown, his dark hair looking equally dishevelled. 'May I enter?'

'Mr Chen. Of course you can,' Luke said, and beckoned him over. 'Have you and your wife chosen names for these two little beauties?'

'Amy and Zoe,' he said with a shy smile. 'Lisa said that they were going to be completely identical to look at so she didn't want to give them similar names.'

'So you chose one from each end of the alphabet. You can't get much more different than that,' Luke said with a chuckle.

Lee Chen leant towards his little daughters, very careful not to touch anything.

'Are they both well? The doctor said before the operation started that Zoe was growing weaker because she couldn't get enough oxygen.'

'Well, they're both getting plenty of oxygen now that we've put the tubes in,' Luke said reassuringly. 'Sahru and Cassie will be looking after them now, and will be keeping a check on your daughters' breathing, their heart-beat and everything else.'

Cassie tuned out everything but the sound of Luke's soothing tone as he explained what he'd found on the ultrasound scan, and she found herself smiling, too, when he presented Lee Chen with his daughters' first photo-graph.

'May I show this to Lisa, my wife?'

'You can give it to her with our compliments,' Luke told him. 'It will be more difficult for her than for other mothers who can have their babies beside them and can show them off to the visitors. This way, at least she will have a photograph to look at when she can't be down here with them, and she can show it to her visitors.'

'In the photograph…' He hesitated and Cassie saw the glitter of repressed tears. 'It just looks as if there is noth-ing wrong with them,' he finished in a rush, then looked almost guilty at having said the words.

'They *are* very beautiful, aren't they?' she agreed softly. 'You can already see how thick and dark their hair will be and their little faces are absolutely perfect.'

Luke must have picked up on the fact that she was trying to accentuate the positive aspects of what had to be a very frightening situation for a new father because he joined in.

'Their little bodies are almost perfect, too, and by the time they've been separated the only thing that will look different from any other set of twins will be a scar on each of their stomachs.'

'Then you will have to start worrying about chasing round after *two* little girls instead of one,' Sahru added and made them all chuckle.

There was a spring in Cassie's step as she made her way out of the unit next day which wasn't entirely due to the good progress Amy and Zoe were making.

Luke had called half an hour previously to confirm that she was still willing to help him with what had been dubbed 'slum clearance'. He had promised that he would be waiting outside the hospital's main entrance when she came off duty, and as she emerged through the automatic doors her eyes were already darting about in search of him.

A piercing whistle drew her attention to his beckoning hand but, to her embarrassment, it seemed as if it also drew the attention of everyone else within a mile's radius of the temporary-waiting bay.

Cassie's cheeks were still flaming as she scrambled into the car and quickly shut the door.

'Did you have to do that?' she scolded.

'I didn't think you'd seen me.'

'Well, you certainly made sure that several dozen people knew you were waiting for me,' she grumbled. 'That'll be all over the hospital by the time I start my next shift, and you can bet that the tale will have grown with the telling.'

'So?' He was concentrating on getting out of the way of an incoming car without knocking over the elderly lady hobbling across in front of him.

'For goodness' sake, Luke! You know what the hospital grapevine's like. We have to work together and I couldn't bear it to have everyone watching us all the time. That's one of the reasons I've always avoided going out with colleagues.' She certainly couldn't tell him that the main reason was Luke himself.

'So, if you haven't been going out with colleagues, who *have* you been going out with?' he asked with a total disregard for her concerns.

'None of your business,' she snapped. 'Anyway, that's not the point. I just don't like the idea of being the focus of everyone's gossiping tongue.' She was gratified when he fell silent but then regretted that she'd put such a dampener on the day.

They were only halfway to his house when he pulled over to the side of the road and turned to face her.

'I'm sorry. I didn't realise that it would embarrass you so much, or I'd never have done it,' he said with quiet contrition. 'Does this mean you'd rather not help me any more?'

She looked at his shadowed eyes and was struck by guilt. When she remembered what he was fighting for her complaint seemed so petty that she found that she just couldn't hang onto her anger any more.

'I'll come and help you on one condition,' she temporised.

'Name it. Anything!' he promised fervently.

'You have to go down on your knees and pray that something monumental comes up to take everyone's mind off you whistling at me,' she ordered imperiously, and was delighted to watch the shadows vanish in a chuckle.

'Come up and see how far I've got,' he invited when the front door had swung closed behind them.

He set off up the stairs, his longer legs taking them two at a time.

She hadn't realised that he'd been unbuttoning his shirt until she reached the top of the stairs and found him stripping it off.

'I started work in Jenny's room,' he continued, apparently completely unaware that the sight of all that naked male flesh was making her fingers tingle with the desire to find out if it was as firm and smooth as it looked.

Last time she'd seen him he'd been covered in cuts from flying glass and twisted metal, although they were hardly noticeable now. All she could see was that the scattering of tawny hairs that stretched from one flat male nipple to the other almost completely concealed the evidence of his injuries. And as for the rest of his body…

Her eyes travelled over him as he turned away, almost as if he were inviting her to examine him, and she took advantage of the opportunity.

He didn't have the over-developed musculature of someone who pumped iron but the sort of lean power that made her think of a predatory animal, sinew, bone and muscle ready in an instant to leap after its prey and—

'Well? What do you think?' he demanded suddenly and she could have groaned. She certainly hadn't been spending the last couple of minutes thinking about the new decorating he'd done in his little daughter's bedroom.

'She's going to love it,' Cassie said hastily as she took a quick look at the gentle peaches-and-cream colour scheme with the parade of rabbits gambolling right around the room.

'All the paint should be dry by now. That means there's just the curtains to hang and the furniture stacked out in the hallway to carry back in and then it's finished.'

'Do you need my help with that or is there something else you'd prefer me to do?'

'Actually…' He paused with a grimace and she groaned.

'What is it? Something completely grisly? Let me guess—the kitchen?'

She could tell from his expression that she'd guessed right and she groaned again.

'You're really stretching friendship to the limits, Luke Thornton,' she warned. 'What have I got to do down there?'

'I've scrubbed everything out so it's mostly just a case of unpacking the last of the boxes and putting things away. Except I haven't a clue where they ought to go,' he admitted.

'Surely you need to do that job yourself if you're going to be using them,' she pointed out.

'I've found enough things so that I can cook myself a meal but there's all the rest of it, all the gadgets and things that you don't use very often but you think that they're absolutely essential when you need them. Anyway, if you remember, you'd already decided that my cupboards needed organising last time you were here.'

Cassie cringed when she remembered the way she'd just blithely rearranged the tins in his cupboard without so much as a by your leave, but Dot's training was too well engrained for her to be able to resist the challenge.

'All right. I'll give it a go,' she agreed, turning back when she reached the door to issue a warning. 'Just don't blame me if you can't find a single thing you want when I've finished.'

There were lots of intriguing thumps and bangs from upstairs while she was getting to grips with the reorganisation of all Luke's cupboards and drawers. The trouble was, what she really wanted to be doing was working side by side with Luke so that she could share in the preparation of his daughter's room.

'Pathetic!' she muttered, and made herself concentrate just a little bit harder on her goal.

She had just set the kettle to boil for a reviving cup of

coffee when she thought she heard a phone ring somewhere in the house, but the noise stopped so quickly that she realised she must have been mistaken.

It was very satisfying to stand back when the job was done and see all the gleaming work surfaces free of clutter, knowing that the insides of each cupboard were just as clean and tidy.

She reached for a pair of sturdy mugs and set them on the smallest tray with one of the collection of packets of chocolate biscuits she'd unearthed.

She made her careful way up the stairs and along the corridor and she was reaching out her free hand to push the door of Jenny's room open when she suddenly realised that everything had gone very quiet.

The door swung open on silent hinges to reveal Luke slumped forward in an old-fashioned rocking chair with his head cradled in his hands.

CHAPTER SIX

'LUKE, what's the matter? What happened?' Cassie demanded in a shocked voice.

Careless of the coffee slopping out of the cups and into the tray to form a moat around the packet of biscuits, she hastily dumped it on top of the chest of drawers and hurried towards him.

He looked up at her, seeming almost to move in slow motion, but even when his eyes met hers they didn't seem to *see* her. With an urgency which was more emotional than professional she noted that there was a film of clammy perspiration across his forehead and he looked as if he was on the verge of passing out.

'Luke?' She knelt down in front of him and took his hands in hers. 'What's the matter? Did you hit your head?'

'No.' He began to shake his head and winced, closing his eyes in obvious pain. 'God, my head hurts,' he groaned.

'Do you know why?' Worried thoughts were whirling round inside her head. What had brought this on? Did he suffer from migraines? Was it evidence of rocketing blood pressure? Perhaps it was a brain tumour? The list of possibilities seemed to grow with each second.

'Probably a combination of things,' he admitted grimly, his voice limited to a low monotone. 'Stress, unaccustomed physical exercise, phone calls from lawyers—take your pick.' He squinted briefly at her out of slitted eyes then closed them again. 'It's been happening at intervals ever since the accident.'

'Did you tell your doctor about it?' she demanded, a whole new list of possibilities rearing up to frighten her. Had he been scanned after the accident or had he been left with undiagnosed but potentially lethal damage to his brain? Was the pain a symptom of a bleed inside the cranium? Perhaps it was a warning that he was about to suffer a stroke?

'Yes, Sister Mills. I've been thoroughly poked prodded and pictured,' he confirmed tiredly. 'There's no evidence of anything organically wrong with me.'

'Except for this pain,' she added. 'Were you given anything for it?'

'Yes. Tablets supposedly strong enough to knock out a horse but, as you can see, they're not very effective.'

As far as Cassie could tell, whatever he'd taken didn't seem to be working at all. His face was positively grey and his eyes looked almost bruised.

'Can you stand up?' she asked, rising to her feet and taking hold of his hands.

'Only if I absolutely have to,' he growled. 'It makes the thumping in my head worse and sometimes movement makes me throw up. Why?'

'I want to get you in the other room to lie down on your bed.'

He was silent for a second, as though digesting her suggestion, and then she heard a pained chuckle. 'You do choose the most inappropriate moment to seduce a man, Cassie Mills. I'm afraid I won't be much good to you at the moment.'

A sudden heated image of the two of them sprawled in wild abandon flashed through Cassie's mind but she ruthlessly suppressed it. If Luke hadn't been half out of his mind with pain she doubted if he'd ever have made such a joke, so it was nothing to get excited about.

'What a good job I was only intending to help you with your headache, then,' she retorted, hoping he couldn't hear the ragged edge to her voice.

She tugged on his hands to pull him up out of the chair.

'Breathe out as you stand up, rather than holding your breath,' she advised. 'It can help to minimise the thumping in your head.'

He was slightly unsteady on his feet and, in spite of her wariness about getting too close to him, she couldn't help offering him the support of an arm around his waist as she guided him into the room next door.

'Sit down,' she ordered when she'd positioned him beside the big rumpled bed and removed her supporting arm.

'Good dog, sit,' he muttered as he lowered himself gingerly on the edge.

Swiftly removing his paint-splattered trainers, she lifted his feet and swivelled them around so that they ended up on his pillow.

'Wrong way,' he muttered, his eyes firmly closed.

'Except it makes it easier to do this,' she murmured as she knelt at the foot of the bed and tentatively ran the tips of her fingers through the thick strands of his hair as she began to massage his skull.

He groaned aloud and she froze.

'Too much?' she asked quickly. 'Tell me if there are any areas where you can't bear the pressure, and I'll avoid them. I don't want to make it worse.'

'Don't stop,' he groaned, laying one hand on top of hers briefly. 'Please, don't stop.'

For nearly half an hour she worked her way silently and systematically over his skull and then down his neck and into his shoulders. Gradually, she felt the knots of tension releasing until finally she realised that he had fallen asleep.

With a slow sigh she sat back on her heels and let her aching hands rest on her thighs. She would probably pay for it tomorrow with sore muscles in her own shoulders and arms, but it was worth it to have been able to ease Luke's pain.

For several minutes she allowed herself the luxury of watching him sleep, his thick lashes giving him the innocent look of a child now that the lines of tension had been soothed away.

His mid-brown hair was ruffled after the massage, sticking up all over in endearing spikes and curls which were usually brushed into submission when he was at work.

His clothing was every bit as disreputable as hers, obviously chosen for its suitability for the messy task in hand rather than its glamour, but that didn't detract from the body inside. In fact, the T-shirt worn paper-thin and the faded jeans probably showed off more intimate details of his well-made body than smarter, newer clothes would have.

Gradually, her interest widened to take in the slightly scruffy look that told her this was one of the rooms that hadn't been touched yet. In fact, the only things which she thought would be worth keeping were the articles of plain solid wooden furniture partly buried under piles of half-emptied boxes.

The sight of those boxes reminded her of the reason she was here in his house at all, and she silently crept out of the room, pulling the door shut behind her. Just because he wasn't in a fit state to work wasn't a reason why she couldn't do her part.

By the time she heard Luke moving about again Cassie had set to with a will.

Jenny's bedroom was completely ready now, with her little cot made up with fresh sheets and a soft furry rabbit waiting for love. There was a mobile of rabbits and carrots circling gently above it as the matching curtains fluttered in the breeze from the open window.

Both the bathroom and Luke's bedroom needed attention but as she hadn't wanted to risk waking him up until he'd slept the headache off she'd moved downstairs to tackle the grisly sitting room.

'Cassie! You're still here!' Luke exclaimed when he appeared in the doorway. 'I can't believe how long I've slept. I was certain you must have given up and gone home hours ago.'

'I had energy to spare and this looked like a good way to use it up,' she said, unaccountably stirred by the rusty edge to his sleepy voice. His eyes were heavy, too, but this time she couldn't see the shadow of pain darkening them. 'Feeling better?'

'Immeasurably! Now I'm just starving. When I woke up I'd been dreaming that I could smell chicken casserole. Now all I can smell is paint.'

Cassie laughed aloud. 'It wasn't a dream. I hope you don't mind, but I raided your freezer so there would be something ready when you woke.'

'You're a star!' he said gratefully. 'Is it ready now?'

'Should be. Go and look while I finish off this corner.'

Luke glanced quickly at what she was doing then took a slower, longer look around.

'Wow, what a transformation. How long was I asleep, for heaven's sake? You've nearly finished the whole room.'

Cassie didn't need to look at her watch to know just

how long it had taken her to scrub the ceiling and walls and apply almost two complete coats of paint. At least there hadn't been much furniture to get in the way, with everything stored in the dining room next door.

'There's still the woodwork to do,' she pointed out as she loaded the roller again. 'And I hope you don't mind that I didn't ask you what colours you wanted to use in here.'

'I was just going to do the whole thing white, to save time, but this looks much better. Warmer,' he added as he took in the contrast between the white ceiling and the softly tinted walls. 'Where did you get the paint? I'm sure I didn't buy this colour. It's rather unusual—a sort of soft, faded terracotta.'

'I mixed several colours from the collection of old paints you'd amassed into a tin of white and took it from there. A designer original,' she quipped.

'It looks good—heaps better than it was before. All it needs now is curtains and some new furniture.'

'Actually, I've had some ideas about that, too,' she volunteered.

'Well, you've done enough for today,' he declared firmly. 'As soon as you've finished that corner you're going to put the roller down and eat. I didn't ask you to come here with the intention of leaving it all to you.'

Cassie was filled with a quiet glow of satisfaction when she finally climbed down from the ladder and stood back to look.

'You've worked miracles,' Luke murmured unexpectedly in her ear as he wrapped his arms around her and gave her a swift squeeze. 'Now come and wash your hands. The food is ready.'

Luke had already served the meal out on two plates and placed a bowl of salad on the table.

'Fruit juice, fizz or coffee,' he offered as she took her place at the temporary dining table squashed into one corner of the kitchen.

The meal began with Luke exclaiming over the amount of work she had packed into the day—he'd had a chance to catch up on her efforts in Jenny's room by now—and her disclaimer that she'd done too much. She deflected his gratitude with a discussion of the jobs still to be done and several suggestions for an inexpensive re-vamp of his existing furnishings.

But even though she thought they were enjoying spending time together, gradually the conversation lapsed as he grew more and more silent and preoccupied.

Cassie was beginning to think she'd outstayed her welcome but was loath to leave him when he was surrounded by such a visible air of depression.

She was certain that she hadn't said anything to cause his change of mood and realised that his thoughts must have returned to the Paynes' threat to take his precious daughter away.

Suddenly she remembered something he'd said when she'd found him in Jenny's room in such pain.

'Luke, what were you saying earlier when your headache was so bad? Something about phone calls from lawyers?'

It looked as if it was almost a physical effort to drag his thoughts to her question, then he grimaced.

'I've a feeling *that* conversation was the final straw that brought on the headache,' he admitted wearily. 'It was confirmation that the Paynes' representative has made the formal application to court on their behalf for sole custody of Jenny.'

'Oh, Luke,' she murmured, feeling his pain as if it were her own. Now that she'd met Jenny and had been captivated by her cheerful smiles and engaging little habits, she could understand why Luke was so despondent.

'Apparently, they've graciously pointed out in their application that I'm a single man working long hours at a demanding job that doesn't pay very well. They say I could be called out at any time of the day or night if one of the patients needs me. Of course, that would mean that I would have to drag Jenny to the hospital with me, rain or shine, if I didn't have any live-in help. Either that or rely on finding instant babysitters who might not care for her the way she should be cared for.'

'Do they know that there's a crèche at the hospital for the staff so that they don't have to worry about unsuitable child care?'

'It wouldn't make any difference to them if they did. As far as they're concerned, only a fully qualified nanny in a uniform full of starch is going to be good enough, and according to them I don't make enough to employ one.'

'So it all comes down to money, does it?' she demanded in disgust. 'Just because they've got plenty, that means they have the right to take your daughter away?'

Ever since he'd first told her about it, Cassie had carefully avoided allowing herself to think too deeply about the situation in case it resurrected old ghosts of her own past. She'd tried to forget the fact that Luke's happiness, and that of his little daughter, was in the hands of some faceless legal person, someone who knew neither of them and probably didn't even care how they felt.

Her heart started to pound and her hands began to shake as the old feeling of helplessness rose up to swamp her.

It had been years since she'd suffered one of these episodes but suddenly she was overcome with a mixture of anger and powerlessness.

She'd been through a version of this herself many years ago but the feeling of vulnerability had never left her. It had been the awful realisation that it hadn't really mattered what she'd wanted, that dreadful old man with the stringy hair and bad breath was going to be the one to decide where she was going to live and with whom.

'Cassie?'

'It's not *fair*, Luke,' she exploded, her hands clenched into tight fists. 'You love Jenny and she obviously loves you. She's your daughter and she belongs with you.'

'Yes, but—' he began, but she steamrollered over him, the words unstoppable once they'd begun to flow.

'Oh, I know that the Paynes have lost *their* daughter and I'm sad for them, but that doesn't give them the right to steal yours. And if the judge can't see that, then there's something wrong with the law.'

She had to stop then because her eyes were flooding with tears and her throat was closing up.

'Hey, Cassie…' He reached across to cradle her cheek in one hand, his thumb gently brushing away the first tear as it escaped to trickle down her face. 'It hasn't happened yet, and my solicitor is investigating all sorts of loopholes and delaying tactics to give me enough time to get my life back on track. I'm not giving up hope that I'll win in the end.'

'What loopholes? What delaying tactics?' she demanded. 'You told me yourself that the Paynes probably had more money than God. They'll probably be able to *buy* the result they want.'

'Not necessarily,' he said firmly. 'I'll certainly be firing off a few shots of my own—such as the fact that they're too old and set in their ways to be able to do the best for a very young child. Even the nanny they've chosen is more like a grandmother than a mother, and she'll certainly be lacking as a playmate. The Paynes are certainly well able to offer her the sort of advantages that cold hard cash can buy, but there's more than having sufficient money to bringing up a happy child.'

Cassie drew in a shaky breath. She was still filled with the remnants of her own remembered misery but his reasoned words went some way towards calming her, as did the hand curled around hers.

'So, what sort of strategies did your solicitor suggest?'

'He stressed how important it was to get the house sorted out as soon as possible, in case the court does appoint a caseworker to look into my home situation. I've also got to investigate all the minute-to-minute mechanics of coping with a little girl while trying to work full time so I've got all the alternatives at my fingertips.'

'You mean, you need to sort out babysitting and a place at the hospital crèche and so on?'

'That, and then there's the possibility that I might have to apply to cut down my hours to part time so that I can spend enough time with her.'

'It's no more than many single mums have to do, I suppose,' Cassie conceded. 'But how would that sit with the hospital? Would they let you drop your hours? Would they be able to find another person willing to work part time to complement your hours, or would they rather get rid of you completely and replace you with someone who can work full time?'

Her heart had dropped like a stone at the thought that Luke might have to leave St Augustine's. Just the thought that he might have to move to another hospital, that she might never see him again…

'I hope not,' he said fervently. 'I like my job and don't

want to move, but if it makes the difference between having Jenny and losing her to the Paynes…'

He didn't need to finish the thought. Cassie knew what his choice would be and could almost feel jealous of the tiny mite for having such a devoted father when her own hadn't been able to hide the fact that his burning wish had been to get rid of her.

'What other choices did he come up with?' she asked, and saw a strange expression cross his face.

He was silent for a moment, almost as if he was debating whether to continue the conversation, then he withdrew his comforting hand from hers and lifted his chin a fraction as though he was bracing himself.

'He suggested I get married,' he said bluntly, and Cassie's heart stopped for several beats before starting to race at warp speed.

'Married?' she squeaked in a strangled voice. 'What does he expect you to do—magically produce a wife out of thin air? Does he expect you to have a candidate already lined up in the wings ready to step centre-stage? And what about the effect on the Paynes if you were to marry again? Wouldn't they be able to accuse you of rushing into something…not treating their daughter's memory with enough reverence?'

Cassie ran out of reasons why the suggestion was a bad one, except for the one she could never voice—that she would hate to see him married to someone else.

Suddenly her emotions were in turmoil.

For two years she'd had to live with the realisation that, because he'd loved Sophie instead of her, he was forever lost to her. Now she faced the prospect of seeing the man she loved marry someone else for the sake of his precious daughter, and her determination to be someone's one and only love didn't seem quite so important if there was a chance that she could be a part of Luke's life.

Then she remembered the endless grey days when she'd had to live with a succession of people who hadn't really cared about her any more than to see that she'd been fed and clothed. She remembered what it was like to live in a house with people who had never praised her or comforted her, had never spoken a single loving word, and she knew that her decision to wait for a man who really loved her had been the right one.

She remembered the little saying she'd found a few years ago and put in a small frame where she could see it from her bed.

To love is nothing.

To be loved is something.

To love and be loved is everything.

Once she'd seen that, she'd known that she was never going to be satisfied with less than everything.

'I don't even know whether I'd be able to find someone willing to marry me,' Luke said quietly. 'I've already been round that block once and had no intention of doing it again, so I know it would be a lot to ask. Why would someone agree to marry me, knowing there was going to be a court battle to gain custody of a child that wasn't even theirs?'

'There must be someone you can ask,' she said weakly, hating the fact that their friendship forced her to encourage him to do something that would hurt her so much. 'You're an attractive man and there's no shortage of female staff at the hospital fighting to catch your attention.'

'So you think I'm attractive, do you?' he questioned with an unexpected glint in his eye as he captured both of her hands in his. 'How attractive, Cassie? Am I attractive enough for *you* to marry me?'

'Me?' she gasped, shocked by the startling turn of events. She tried to retrieve her hands but he wouldn't release her. 'No, Luke. Definitely not,' she declared, trying to be firm while her heart somersaulted with 'if onlys'.

'Please, Cassie,' he said, leaning towards her persuasively so that his deep voice flowed around her like dark honey. 'You're my best chance, as well as being the most believable one. We've been working together for over two years now, and we've built up a good rapport. I don't know what else to do to stack the deck in my favour. If I let the Paynes win even the first round of the battle, I'll stand less and less chance of winning the war.'

Cassie knew he was right. She'd seen enough of the results of such lost battles during her own time in foster-care. 'But, Luke, marriage…?'

Oh, she was tempted. He would never know how tempted she was to accept his proposal without a single reservation, in spite of her long-held beliefs.

After all, who would she be hurting if she accepted?

It wasn't as if Luke was divorced with an ex-wife and family to support. She wouldn't have to share him with anyone except his daughter and any children they might eventually have together. And if, over time, he came to love her even half as much as she'd loved him for the last two years, then her gamble would have paid off.

Her heart was pounding and she wanted to cross her fingers as she drew in a steadying breath to still her frantic thoughts long enough to accept his proposal.

'It could be a temporary arrangement,' he offered into the fraught silence before she could speak, releasing her hands and straightening away from her. 'That's if you didn't want to make it a permanent thing—and there's no reason why you would, after all.'

'Temporary?' she repeated woodenly, her hands suddenly cold without his holding them as her fragile castles in the air came crashing around her ears.

'Only the two of us would know that, of course,' he added quickly, leaning towards her again. 'As far as everyone else was concerned, it would have to be real.'

Cassie felt a little sick and wrapped her arms protectively around herself, not certain what to think.

She'd been so sure that Luke was actually offering her a real marriage. For a moment she was sure she'd seen something special in his eyes, or had that only been wishful thinking on her part?

'Please, Cassie. Just until Jenny's mine again.'

The ache of longing in his voice reminded her of the real point of the whole conversation, but it also brought up other aspects they hadn't discussed.

'We could hardly file for a divorce as soon as she was handed over to you. I can just see the in-laws from hell letting you get away with that.'

'So, what's your point?'

'I'm saying that the marriage wouldn't be just until you secured permanent custody of Jenny,' she explained doggedly. 'It would have to go on for months longer than that to avoid suspicion, and in those months I would be spending a lot of time with your daughter.'

She fixed him with a steely glare honed from too many losses in her own life. 'Have you thought about Jenny's feelings in all your plans? If she bonds with me as a substitute mother, how will she feel when we divorce and I go out of her life? She was probably too young to realise what happened to Sophie but she'll be that much older when I go.'

'You'll still be working at St Augustine's and we'll still be friends, so she'll still see you,' he said with simple masculine logic that took little notice of any emotional entanglement.

'Anyway,' he added with apparent nonchalance, 'who's to say that we won't decide in the meantime to make it a permanent thing?'

That he would even be willing to consider the possibility was a temptation in itself.

Everything she'd wanted when she'd first met him two years ago was within her reach...except that she hadn't been his first choice. He'd loved Sophie rather than her. The relationship he was proposing between the two of them wouldn't even be a real marriage, just a device which his solicitor had hinted would help him to get custody of his precious Jenny.

She could understand how eager he was to persuade her to go along with his plan, but how likely was his suggestion that the relationship might become permanent? Would a wife he didn't love just become nothing more than an inconvenience once Jenny was his?

Cassie could remember all too clearly when her own parents had seen her as nothing more than a nuisance and had sworn that it would never happen to her again.

Marriage was a risky enough proposition without a hidden agenda. If she couldn't be anyone's one and only, she would be a fool to try to walk that tightrope at all.

But she cared for Luke, far more than she'd ever admit to a living soul. How would she ever forgive herself if he lost his daughter to the in-laws from hell and she could have prevented it? It would break his heart, especially after losing Sophie.

'Please, Luke, my head is spinning. Let me have some time to think about it,' she temporised weakly, torn in every direction.

'How much time?' he asked. 'Only things seem to be

moving pretty fast with the Paynes' money behind them, so we can't afford to leave it too long or the marriage won't be credible. As it is, the Paynes' solicitor will almost certainly accuse me of marrying you in haste purely to tip the scales in my direction.'

'You mean they're probably going to be suspicious no matter what we say or do? Oh, Luke, I don't think I'd be any good at lying to people if they started interrogating me.'

'Oh, Cassie…' Luke closed his eyes and his shoulders slumped for a moment before he looked at her again with the light of burning desperation in his gaze. '*Please*, don't let them take my Jennywren away.'

Cassie had to swallow hard to get rid of the large lump that had suddenly taken up residence in her throat. How was she supposed to be able to resist him when he looked at her like that, with his heart in his eyes?

'Luke, don't… I can't…' she began incoherently, hardly able to put two words together when her emotions were in such a tangle.

It was such a crazy, impossible thing to do and she should be turning him down without a second thought, but when she remembered the look of devotion on Luke's face when he'd cradled his daughter in his arms fresh from her bath…

'Oh, dammit! All right, Luke, I'll do it,' she snapped irritably. 'But don't you dare let anyone know that it's not—'

She never got to finish her sentence before Luke had swept her up out of her chair and into his arms with a whoop of joy.

'Yes! Yes! Yes!' he exclaimed exultantly, and laughed as he swung her around the tight confines of the kitchen in an exuberant dance. 'Oh, Cassie, thank you a thousand times…a million times! I promise you won't regret it.'

Cassie was already regretting it.

The feel of his arms around her was something she'd only dreamed about when her rigid control slipped. For two years, ever since Luke and Sophie had become an item, she'd tried to banish her feelings towards him and she was only now realising how futile the effort had been.

To be this close to him, their bodies pressed together from shoulder to knee, told her that he was every bit as strong, every bit as virile and masculine as she'd imagined. Her memories of his bruised and battered body in a hospital bed hadn't done him justice.

Unfortunately for her peace of mind, his open delight at her agreement to his proposal only served to make him more attractive. If this was how she felt now, how much more attached to him would she be in a week, a month, a year? How would she avoid falling fathoms deep in love with him all over again only to have to learn how to survive without him when the marriage came to an end?

'We need to make plans,' he declared when he finally lowered her feet to the floor.

She tried to step back out of his arms, needing to break the connection if her brain was ever going to work again, but he wouldn't release her. One arm was firmly wrapped around her shoulders as he turned towards the door.

'Let's sit in the sitting room while we talk,' he suggested, but she didn't really feel that he left her much choice. It seemed almost as if she'd strayed into the path of some irresistible force of nature and had no option but to submit. 'Pull up a seat,' he said as he flipped the paint-splattered cloth out of the way and sank onto the carpet beneath.

Tethered to him by one hand, she copied his position,

coming to rest at last with her back against a now dry freshly painted wall.

'I suggest we get married in the hospital chapel,' he began, his mind obviously whirling at the speed of light as he spoke. 'In spite of the fact that it's not very long since Sophie died, we'll need to make a bit of a do about it by inviting a few friends and colleagues, otherwise it would look suspicious. And, don't forget, everyone must believe it's real.'

'What, even Kirstin and Naomi?' She couldn't imagine not telling her two friends the truth, and when she remembered that Naomi was in the middle of planning her own wedding at the moment she couldn't help but contrast the two events.

'*Especially* Kirstin and Naomi,' he said firmly. 'They're the first people the Paynes' legal eagles would pump for information if they're trying to use the marriage against us in the custody fight.'

The thought of lying to her friends was suddenly very depressing. The three of them had been there for each other for so many years now that they were probably closer than most sisters. Trying to keep such a secret would be bound to affect the complicated bonds between them.

What would she do if the relationship didn't recover, even when she was at liberty to explain the reason why? As well as losing Luke and Jenny, she would also have lost her two closest friends.

Unfortunately, she understood only too well why it would have to be that way. Neither she nor Luke could afford to give anyone the ammunition the Paynes needed.

'Tomorrow we need to buy you a ring,' he continued briskly, and she felt uncomfortably like a rabbit caught in the glare of a bright light. Now that she'd agreed, he was probably unstoppable. It seemed as if she didn't even need to speak; he was taking her agreement almost for granted.

'Cassie? Would you rather choose your own ring?' he suggested softly, and, just like that, he'd snapped her out of her doldrums.

'That's not necessary if we're in a hurry,' she said, suddenly feeling guilty that she was having such negative thoughts. If she'd agreed to their marriage—and she had—then in all fairness she ought to be doing her share of working out what needed to be done.

'We're not in so much of a hurry that we can't take the time to find the ring you want,' he said, his eyes very clear as he met her gaze. 'I'll phone one of the jewellers in town and set up an appointment to view, then we won't have to make any decisions with other customers jostling around us.'

He was silent for a long moment after she'd murmured her startled agreement, his eyes travelling over her face and her hair almost as if he were seeing her for the first time.

She was very aware that her streaky blonde hair was tumbling haphazardly out of the ponytail which had held it out of her eyes for the painting. It had undoubtedly collected a few extra streaks of brilliant white and customised pale terracotta. Her face was probably liberally spattered with paint, too, and her clothes were far from glamorous, but there was no trace of dismay evident on his face when he looked at her.

'Diamonds,' he murmured as he lifted one hand to brush aside a straggly tendril of hair, his fingertip just brushing the skin of her cheek and sending an electric shiver through her. 'Diamonds set in gold would suit you perfectly. Beautiful, traditional and very, very classy.'

CHAPTER SEVEN

'OH, WOW, Cassie, that's beautiful,' Naomi cried when she grabbed her hand for a closer look at the ring. 'It's absolutely perfect for you.'

'Let me see,' Kirstin demanded as she elbowed Naomi out of the way just as she had when they'd been argumentative teenagers. 'Oh, yes. Classic good taste. Did you choose it or did he? It must have cost a fortune.'

'I've no idea how much it cost—Luke wouldn't tell me—and we chose it together,' she said staunchly. She deliberately ignored the fact that when they'd arrived at the shop he'd evidently already primed the jeweller with the information that they only wanted to look at diamonds set in gold.

At the last moment he'd obviously had a qualm of conscience and had actually asked her if she'd rather have a coloured stone instead, but by then she'd fallen in love with this ring and nothing would have changed her mind.

Still, she thought as she admired the elegant solitaire adorning her hand, she'd been gratified that he'd actually offered her the ultimate choice, even if she still felt desperately guilty for the reason she was wearing a ring in the first place.

'What do *you* think of it, Dot?' Naomi demanded, as she gazed down with proprietorial pride at the cluster of diamonds surrounding a single sapphire. 'It's so different from mine.' Cassie braced herself to turn and face the woman whose approval meant most.

'It's a very beautiful ring,' her former foster-mother

said softly, her faded blue-grey eyes full of the wisdom of the world as she fixed them unblinkingly on Cassie's. 'It's a perfect symbol of the relationship between you and Luke.'

A sudden shiver ran up Cassie's spine at her words. On the surface, she seemed to be referring to the saying 'Diamonds are forever' but she was obviously trying to convey a deeper meaning with her eyes than either Naomi or Kirstin recognised, and it made Cassie uncomfortable.

Had Dot guessed the real reason behind this sudden engagement and the wedding they were planning in just two short weeks? Was she tacitly commenting on the fact that the ring was no more than surface glitter, a mere triviality when set against the solid worth of a strong bond between a truly committed couple? Was she trying to warn her that they were making a mistake or would Dot understand if she realised that they were doing it with the best of intentions?

How she wished she could confide in the woman who had been more of a mother to her than her own mother had been, pour out her fears the way she'd been able to ever since she'd realised that, unlike her parents, Dot would never abandon her.

'Come here and let me give you a hug,' Dot demanded as she opened her arms to Cassie. 'All I can wish for you is that you and your Luke will have the same sort of happiness in your marriage that Arthur and I found.'

'Oh, Dot,' Cassie whispered against the silvery halo of hair, almost speechless with guilt as she tightened her arms around the slender shoulders of the older woman.

She knew she was wishing for the impossible. How could she and Luke ever be as happy as Dot and Arthur when they weren't even starting off with love on both sides, when the whole marriage was nothing more than a sham to prevent his daughter being taken away from him?

'Shall I go out to the shop on the corner and see if I can find us a celebratory bottle of bubbly?' Naomi offered, her cheerful voice cutting through Cassie's uncomfortable thoughts.

'There's no need. I've already got a decent one in the fridge,' Dot said smugly. 'As soon as Cassie phoned this morning to tell me that all three of you were coming to visit this evening, I knew there was going to be something special to celebrate. The glasses are all set out on the side, washed and polished, and I've put a few of your favourite nibbles out, too.'

Kirstin and Naomi whooped gleefully as they rushed towards the kitchen, obviously as delighted at the impromptu party as if they'd still been those long ago teenagers.

Part of Cassie ached for nothing more than to take advantage of a couple of minutes alone with Dot. She desperately needed to soak up some of the aura of calm that always surrounded her, but with the uncomfortable burden of guilt bearing down on her she didn't dare. Dot had always had an uncanny sense that told her when one of 'her' girls was up to no good and Cassie was very much afraid that she would see straight through this flimsy charade.

'I'd better lend a hand, especially if I'm going to get a look-in with the goodies,' she said brightly, carefully avoiding Dot's gaze as she made her escape.

'You're *s-o-o* sly!' Kirstin exclaimed when Cassie joined them in the kitchen. 'I was absolutely certain there was something going on between you and Luke but you swore he wasn't even on your list.'

'List! Pooh!' snorted Naomi around a mouthful of

filched food as she tried to fit an extra plate of Dot's special offerings on a tray. 'You can't decide on something like that with an arbitrary list of names. If the right man comes along, it'll be obvious, just like it was for Edward and me. Take Luke, for instance. I can't understand why you were so slow about snapping him up two years ago, before Sophie got her hands on him. He's ideal for you.'

Cassie had thought so, too, but it was interesting to hear that someone else agreed.

'What do you mean, ideal?' she asked, pretending to concentrate on threading her fingers between the stems of the glasses so she wouldn't have to look at anyone. She was suddenly worried that if the others had divined how she really felt about Luke, they could equally have realised that he didn't love her. For Jenny's sake, she needed to know because the pretence *had* to be maintained.

'Well, for a start you've got so much in common, both of you working in the same unit. He seems like a nice man, too, well thought of, *and* his salary will come in very handy when you decide to start that family you've always wanted.'

'He's also rather good-looking, if you're considering the genetic inheritance of your offspring,' Kirstin added cheekily as she gathered up the last of the items Dot had left ready, piling paper serviettes on top of plates and grabbing the bottle of champagne. 'In fact, he's got it all, hasn't he—brains, looks *and* money? What more could a woman ask for?'

'A generous, loving heart,' said a soft voice from the doorway as Dot joined them, obviously having overheard the last part of their conversation. 'You could lose all the rest and still be happy if his heart was in the right place.'

'You're just biased because you were lucky enough to

find Arthur,' teased Naomi, planting a noisy kiss on the soft, papery cheek as she carried her precarious burden past their diminutive mentor. 'Unfortunately, I think he was the last one that came out of that mould. They don't seem to make men like that any more so we girls have to make the best of it.'

'Yes, Dot,' Kirstin chimed in. 'I obviously need help. If you know where I ought to go looking for one of these paragons it's about time you let me know. It's all right for Naomi and Cassie because they've made their choice, but I'm still having to kiss a lot of frogs while I try to find my prince.'

The light-hearted banter continued while they were eating and it was some time later before the conversation returned to the topic of the wedding.

'So, tell us what you've decided about the ceremony,' Naomi quizzed, her eyes shining with as much anticipation as if it had been her own wedding they were talking about. 'Have you decided whether it's going to be a church do or a registry office? You'll have to have an enormous reception if you're going to invite all your colleagues. You're not going to make Kirstin and I dress up like animated meringues, are you? Exactly how long have we got to prepare for this extravaganza, anyway, remembering that it's the end of June now? What a shame there won't be enough time for us to make it a double wedding.'

'It's in the middle of July,' Cassie said quietly when her friend finally stopped bubbling.

'Oh, good. A summer wedding, and we've got a whole year to organise everything,' she said happily.

'No, Naomi,' Cassie interrupted nervously, knowing she'd probably reached the most crucial point in an uncomfortable evening. '*This* July. In two weeks' time.'

'*Two weeks!*' they chorused, and after a stunned pause three pairs of eyes focused simultaneously on her slender waist.

Cassie's cheeks flamed when she suddenly realised what they were thinking—that the reason for the haste was because she'd discovered she was pregnant.

'No! It's not because I'm...because we've... Because we *haven't*!' she declared almost incoherently, hardly knowing where to look in her embarrassment. In her determination to succeed in her career she hadn't had nearly enough practice on the dating scene to be blasé about such a conversation.

'Well, Cassie, love, if you aren't in the family way, why *is* there such a rush?' Dot asked into the silence.

'Probably *because* they haven't done you-know-what, and can't wait!' Naomi teased wickedly, and had her hand swiftly smacked by Dot.

'It's because of Jenny, his daughter,' Cassie explained, frantically trying to remember which parts of the real story she and Luke had agreed on as being safe for general consumption. *Oh, what a tangled web...* 'You probably remember me telling you that he was in a car crash several months ago?'

'Yes, I do. The poor man lost his wife and was badly injured, wasn't he?' Dot said, proving that there was absolutely nothing wrong with her memory in spite of her age.

'Well, he's out of hospital and back at work now, and trying to pick up the pieces of his life, and we—'

'Well, Cassie, I hope he's not just marrying you to have a babysitter for his daughter,' Kirstin interrupted.

'Certainly not!' Cassie exclaimed indignantly, uncomfortably aware that there was actually an element of truth in the situation. 'He could hire a nanny if that was *all* he wanted.'

'So?' Kirstin challenged. 'That still doesn't explain the haste.'

'So Luke and I have been colleagues and friends for two years now, as Naomi kindly pointed out, and we've always got on well. When he was hurt I went to visit him in hospital to find out if he was going to be all right.' She'd only visited him once, but she wasn't telling *them* that. 'Anyway, now that he's back at work and we're seeing each other every day, we've realised that there's always been something more between us and so we decided…'

She wound down like an old-fashioned clock as she ran out of breath and shrugged, waiting for someone to speak.

'And you both realised that there was a special something in the air when you were together, so why not rush into marriage?' Kirstin finished for her with a touch of acid in her voice.

'Yes and no,' Cassie retorted stubbornly, refusing to let her friend get away with the sarcasm. 'Yes, there *is* something special.' Even if it's totally one-sided, she added silently. 'And, no, we don't think we're rushing into anything. We've already known each other for two *years*, for heaven's sake! And then there's Jenny to think about. She's lost her mother and she's hardly seen her father for several months while he's been in hospital. She's nine months old now, so the sooner we get married, the sooner her life can return to normal. She's a beautiful little girl and she needs a father *and* a mother.'

The passion in her final words seemed to reverberate around the room and she suddenly realised that there were some deep issues of her own being resurrected.

Once *she* had been the little girl who'd needed a father and a mother, but her parents hadn't wanted her and she'd ended up being shunted into a system that had treated her more like a number than a heartbroken individual.

She would never stop thanking the sheer good luck that had eventually landed her in Dot's home, and if taking care of Jenny for Luke was her way of paying for that luck, so be it.

'Did his wife have any family?' Dot asked. Predictably, her expression had softened at the mention of Jenny but she was obviously thinking about the other ramifications of the situation.

'Just a father and mother who have been taking care of Jenny while Luke was unable to.'

'How do they feel about him remarrying so soon?' she probed, as ever going straight to the heart of a problem.

'We haven't told them yet,' Cassie admitted, then carefully turned the conversation off that topic. 'We wanted to tell you three first, but Luke is on duty at the moment and the next time we'd be free together Kirstin and Naomi couldn't come.'

She crossed her fingers that she wouldn't have to admit that they were hoping that the Paynes didn't find out about the wedding until much closer to the date. If they did, Luke was very afraid that they would find some way to use the information to stop him from visiting Jenny. After his long stay in hospital he really needed to spend as much time he could with her to strengthen the bonds before they had to face the might of the law.

By the time Cassie locked her front door behind her that night she was physically and mentally exhausted by the tension of the evening.

As usual, she dialled Dot's number and let it ring twice

to signal her safe arrival before she collapsed across the bed with a heartfelt groan.

She groaned again when the phone rang almost immediately and nearly decided not to answer. She didn't really have the energy to keep her brain one step ahead of her tongue if it was Kirstin or Naomi, trying to get another question or two in under her guard.

'Coward!' she muttered at the last moment before the machine cut in to answer for her and she grabbed the receiver.

'Cassie?'

Luke's voice was soft and warm and sent a shiver up her spine almost as if she'd been stroked with a piece of thick soft velvet.

'Oh, Luke, thank goodness it's you,' she groaned in relief, and flopped back against the pillows. 'I nearly let the machine answer because I thought it might be one of the others.'

'I'm sorry, Cassie. Was it bad?'

'Not bad, exactly. More like nerve-racking. You'll understand the first time you meet that trio *en masse*. If the era wasn't wrong, you'd think they'd taught the Spanish Inquisition the tricks of the trade.'

'Poor Cassie,' he said sympathetically. 'Do you want me to come over so you can get it all off your chest or would you prefer to come over here?'

Cassie grew still as her heartbeat suddenly began to race. It was only hours since she'd seen him last but her every instinct was urging her to rush over to be with him.

Exactly when, she wondered, had the mere thought of seeing Luke begun to have this effect on her?

She was going to have to get a grip on her runaway emotions or, when their arrangement finally ended, she was going to end up badly hurt. Her disappointment when

Luke had married Sophie would be nothing in comparison.

'Luke, I'm so shattered I'm going to go straight to bed. Anyway, I daren't come over there in case it's a crafty ploy to get me to do some more work,' she teased.

'It's not that at all. I was only thinking of you,' he protested. 'Besides, I've already packed up for the night. I've actually made a start on the dining room, now that the sitting room furniture's all been moved out, but after the day we had today in the unit I didn't have much stamina left either.'

Of course, then Cassie had to ask what had been going on in the unit in her absence and heard all about the twins who had arrived at only twenty-two weeks' gestation.

'Non-identical, one of each sex,' Luke told her. 'Unfortunately, the little boy didn't make it past six hours—his lungs just weren't up to it, even with surfactant—but his sister's still fighting to stay with us. Hopefully, you'll see her tomorrow.'

Cassie asked for an update on 'her' Siamese twins and was relieved to hear that there were tentative signs that Zoe, the twin with the smaller share of their mutated livers and nutrient-rich blood supply, was beginning to stabilise. Perhaps the extra nutrition she was being given through her IV line would be enough to counteract the effect of the birth anomalies until the two of them grew strong enough to be separated.

'Will you have the time and energy to come over here after work tomorrow?' he asked after a brief pause in the conversation. In the background Cassie could hear music playing and recognised it as the Spanish guitar concerto she'd chosen for them to listen to the last time she was over there, helping with the redecoration.

'Of course,' she agreed, wondering when it had become

essential to spend time with him even though they worked in the same department all day. 'I'll have to come and inspect your efforts to make sure you're keeping the standards up.'

They both chuckled at the reminder of their running dispute over who was the more painstaking decorator and Cassie realised that, whether she was ready for it or not, their relationship was slowly changing.

She'd been so worried that the friendship they'd developed over the last two years would be ruined by their new status. It was such a relief to find that they just seemed to be adding a new dimension to it.

Before she could stifle it she was overcome by a jaw-cracking yawn.

'Oh, Luke, I'm sorry. That wasn't a reflection on the conversation,' she said hastily.

'I'll take your word for it and let you catch up on some sleep,' he sighed with mock despondency. 'I just wanted to let you know that the chapel's been organised and I've invited the solicitor as an unofficial witness.'

Cassie didn't know whether to laugh or cry as she said her goodbyes and put the phone down.

She doubted whether many brides-to-be were told that their prospective groom had booked the venue for their forthcoming nuptials and then, in the same breath, that he'd invited someone from the legal profession to witness them perjuring themselves.

'Do you, Luke Thornton, take Cassandra Mills…'

The time-honoured words surrounded the two of them as they stood in the simple chapel, and Cassie had the strange feeling that any minute now she was going to wake up and find it was all some surreal dream. Not that her dreams had ever gone quite this far before.

It must be someone else standing here beside Luke and preparing to exchange solemn vows, someone else wearing this perfectly simple gown of ivory-coloured silk and carrying a simple spray of cornflowers which exactly matched the blue of his eyes.

A movement beside her drew her bemused gaze up until she met those clear blue eyes.

'I, Luke Thornton, take you, Cassandra Mills…' he repeated, his deep, slightly husky voice as calm and steady as ever. Except for one startled moment Cassie thought she caught a glimpse of something very intent in his eyes and could almost have believed that he meant every word.

A sound from the small gathering of friends behind them brought her to her senses, and then it was her turn to speak.

'I, Cassandra Mills, take you, Luke Thornton…' she began carefully, knowing how important it was for everyone to believe in what they were seeing.

Then her eyes met Luke's again and suddenly she forgot completely that there was anyone in the room besides the two of them.

The whole ceremony might have been deliberately planned to help him gain custody of his daughter, but that fact didn't seem to matter to her heart.

For two years she'd carefully suppressed her feelings towards him and had believed that they'd died. Now, with her hand in his and the time-honoured words on her lips, her emotions burst into fully fledged life again and she knew that she meant every syllable.

'You may now kiss your bride,' said the hospital chaplain, smiling benignly as he closed his book.

Cassie froze.

For some reason she'd completely blocked out the fact that Luke would be expected to kiss her in front of the whole congregation. They'd known each other for two years and the closest they'd ever got, apart from the times when they'd worked side by side, had been the evening when she'd massaged his headache away and when he'd given her that exuberant hug when she'd agreed to this marriage.

She began to tremble as her pulse went into overdrive.

They'd never kissed before and now they were going to have their first attempt in front of more than a dozen pairs of eyes, one of them belonging to his lawyer.

'Relax,' he breathed softly, a reassuring smile on his face and in his eyes as he drew her into his arms. 'Just a peck.'

Mesmerised by the sight of his head angling towards her, she noticed the moment that he closed his eyes, his thick dark lashes forming crescents on his cheekbones just the way they had when she'd watched him sleep.

That was her last thought because that was when his lips touched hers and the rest of the world ceased to exist.

Aeons later, it seemed it was the sound of laughter and a ripple of applause that drew them apart and her only consolation as they were surrounded by their friends was the fact that Luke seemed every bit as stunned as she was.

She'd never realised that a kiss could be like that, although how she would define *that* she had no idea.

It had only been the meeting of two mouths but it had been the most gentle, exhilarating, soothing, arousing, *intimate* thing that had ever happened to her in her life. For a while there it had almost felt as if their souls had touched.

'Save some of that for tonight,' Naomi murmured to the two of them with a wicked grin as she pretended to fan herself. 'For a minute I thought we were going to have to break out the fire extinguishers.'

Cassie felt the heat of a renewed blush flare up her throat and into her face and was surprised to see a darker hue spread over Luke's cheekbones, too.

'Obviously a convincing performance, then,' he murmured in Cassie's ear before he turned to greet another of their well-wishers, and she felt the blood drain towards her feet. His words were almost as shocking as if he'd drenched her with a bucket of ice water.

Was that all it had been to him, that magical meeting of mouths, minds and hearts which she'd been convinced they'd just shared? Had it been nothing more than a convincing performance for a critical audience?

'Congratulations,' said a softly spoken man in a smart grey suit very similar to Luke's. He shook hands with Luke then turned to Cassie and waited to be introduced.

'Cassie, this is Jordan French, the legal eagle I told you about,' Luke said.

'I'm very pleased to meet you, Mrs Thornton,' he said with a smile. 'I don't often get invited to this sort of event. Dealing in family law, it's more usual to find myself in the divorce courts at the other end of a marriage.'

Cassie smiled sickly at him, unable to find a single thing to say. All she could think of was exactly how long it would be before he was sitting down with Luke to organise their own separation. Perhaps an annulment would be unusual enough to make it interesting for him.

'In this case, I've got a proprietary interest,' he continued, obviously unaware of her train of thought. 'I'm taking the credit for telling Luke that if he'd known you so long it was about time he got round to proposing to you. You're entirely too beautiful for him to risk leaving you without a ring on your finger.'

'You wouldn't be trying to sweet-talk my wife, would you, French?' Luke challenged. 'Go and find one of your own. There's a whole hospital full of women through that door.'

'If they're all like Cassie, I might just think about it. I see far too many marriages go wrong to want to leap into anything in a hurry, but seeing the two of you together is almost enough to change my mind.'

He made his excuses then, citing a mountain of paperwork waiting for attention at his office, but Cassie barely heard him. After the emotional overload of the last few minutes it was taking her all her time to stay upright and look intelligent. And there were still several hours to get through at the reception which Dot, Naomi and Kirstin had put together before she could allow her smile to slip.

'I think we were convincing enough,' Luke said as the taxi disappeared on its way back to the rank at the front of the hospital. 'I must say, it's nice to be able to relax and not to have to think about everyone watching our every move.'

Cassie didn't bother to answer, opting instead for making her way as swiftly as her impractical outfit would allow past his car parked in the driveway towards the house. The sooner she was out of the sight of the rest of the world, the happier she would be…and that included Luke.

He put the key in the lock as he joined her by the door and then, before she realised what he was going to do, he swept her off her feet and into his arms in a swirl of ivory silk.

'Luke! What are you doing?' she squeaked as she flung her arms around his neck to hold on.

'Following tradition,' he said with a grin, and stepped over the threshold.

'Don't be silly. Put me down!' she demanded when he swung round to push the door shut without releasing her.

'Must do the job properly,' he declared virtuously as he looked down at her.

Cassie was so tempted to just go with the flow. It felt different and very exciting to be carried like this. She couldn't remember it ever happening before, not even when she'd been small, and to feel Luke's strong arms surrounding her and cradling her as if she were something infinitely precious was very seductive.

Then the small voice of common sense spoke up and reminded her that the fantasy wasn't real. It might seem as if Luke was still holding her close just because he was enjoying holding her, but she'd been wrong about his reactions when he'd kissed her, too.

'You can put me down now,' she said flatly, unwinding her arms from around his neck and trying vainly to hold herself away from him. 'There's no one here to see what we're doing.'

Luke grew still and the teasing smile disappeared.

'As you wish,' he said stiffly, and lowered her feet to the floor.

For a moment his arm stayed wrapped around her shoulders, as though making sure she was steady on her feet, but when she took a hasty step back he allowed it to fall.

'I'll go upstairs and change out of this,' she said, gesturing towards her wedding dress. 'Then I'd better get my things unpacked or I won't be able to find anything in the morning.'

With the wedding taking place at such short notice there had been no possibility of taking time off for a honeymoon, even if theirs had been a real love match. The best they'd been able to arrange had been to take a single day and tell their colleagues that they would be making up for the omission later.

'I'll put the kettle on, then. Would you prefer tea or coffee?' he offered blandly, and she paused partway up the stairs.

He sounded almost as though he were talking to a complete stranger, and it made her heart ache when she compared it to his boyish high spirits of just a few minutes ago. Still, in spite of her momentary lapses whenever he put his arms around her, there was no point in either of them forgetting that theirs wasn't an ordinary marriage. Slipping into the realms of make-believe could only make things more painful in the end.

She would have liked to have refused his offer in the hope that half an hour out of his presence would untangle her muddled emotions. Unfortunately, Naomi and Kirstin had made sure that they'd been toasted up to the hilt at the reception and all the champagne they'd drunk had left her with a raging thirst.

'Tea, please,' she decided. 'Do you want me to come down for it?'

'I'll bring it up in a minute,' he said, and turned towards the kitchen.

Cassie continued upwards and turned automatically towards the third and smallest bedroom. She knew that Luke had been working on it in the days since she'd last been here, but hadn't seen what he'd done.

'Oh!' she exclaimed when she stood in the doorway and saw that the room had been set up as a fully functioning office. Even with a shoehorn she wouldn't be able to fit a bed in here, and with the other two rooms already designated as Jenny's and Luke's…

She whirled and stepped as swiftly as her slender gown would allow across to Luke's door and swung it open.

When she saw her suitcases sitting in front of his newly installed wardrobe the small niggle of disquiet exploded almost instantly into full-blown anger.

How dare he? she fumed as her pulse went haywire and her blood began to simmer. For one wild moment she actually contemplated grabbing the suitcases and flinging them noisily out into the corridor.

He'd been at great pains to make sure she remembered that their marriage was a fake. Immediately after their kiss at the end of the ceremony he'd reminded her that the whole performance had been just for show. Yet here was the evidence that he obviously expected her to make it a real one by sleeping with him! *How dare he?*

The pang of regret that theirs wasn't to be a real marriage was ruthlessly ignored. She'd had plenty of time to absorb the fact that, while she'd always been attracted to Luke, she was nothing more than second best to him.

She heard the sound of footsteps on the stairs and whirled to face him, determined to put him straight once and for all.

'Tea, as requested,' he offered politely. The fact that he seemed to have recovered his own equanimity and was apparently oblivious of her anger only served to wind her up more.

'I've got something rather more pressing on my mind than tea,' she snapped. 'What I'd like to know is why you've presumed to put *my* cases in *your* room. With all your frequent reminders, I know you haven't forgotten that this marriage of ours is only for show. Unfortunately, there's something else you need to remember…with a make-believe marriage, you *don't* get the privileges of the marital bed.'

CHAPTER EIGHT

CASSIE expected Luke to apologise or defend himself but instead he remained utterly silent as he deposited her tea on the corner of the nearest chest of drawers and turned to leave the room.

'Luke!' she snapped, astounded that he would just turn his back and walk away. 'Are you so arrogant that you're just going to ignore me?'

'Certainly not,' he retorted, equally sharply. 'I wouldn't dare.' But he continued on his way towards his daughter's room without even slowing his stride.

'Well, what have you got to say, then?' she persisted. She was unaccountably disappointed in him as she trailed after him along the corridor, but this was something that needed to be sorted out straight away.

Now that they were married, he was certainly showing a completely different side to the Luke she'd thought she's known.

'What have I got to say? Nothing much,' he said, and she almost ploughed into him as he suddenly came to a halt in the middle of his daughter's room and turned to face her. 'Except that it's obvious you didn't make sure of your facts before you leapt to conclusions.'

She'd always thought he was a fairly self-contained man who rarely revealed his private emotions, but over the last few weeks she'd gradually been learning to read his expressions.

At the moment there wasn't a trace of guilt to be seen.

Instead, there was the weary disillusionment of someone who has been let down once too often.

'If you'd waited a moment before you started making assumptions I would have shown you this.' He gestured towards the small, new-looking settee sitting neatly against one freshly painted wall.

Cassie frowned as she gazed around, suddenly realising that something had changed since she'd last seen the room. It looked as if everything had been moved around to clear nearly half of the floor space in front of the settee.

As she watched he bent forward to grasp hold of the front edge of the seat and pulled. In seconds, a small double bed had unfolded in front of her eyes.

His face was still wearing that dreadful closed expression when he straightened up. 'In view of the nature of our arrangement, I took it for granted that you would prefer a measure of privacy,' he said tonelessly.

Cassie felt sick as she realised how unfairly she had judged him, but couldn't find words to begin her abject apology before he continued speaking.

'I thought it would work better if your clothes stayed in my room, as if we're sleeping together like any normal married couple. If this is folded away each day then there will be nothing obvious to tell any nosy in-laws—or anyone else—that we aren't sharing the bed as well.'

'Luke…' Cassie suddenly realised just how much she had hurt him, but couldn't think of any words eloquent enough to tell him how much she regretted it. 'Luke, I'm so sorry. I—'

'No apology necessary,' he said dismissively. 'I'll leave you to get on with your unpacking. Don't forget to drink your tea.' He gave her a wide berth as he started to leave the room.

'Luke, please,' she called, and to her relief he paused

in the doorway then slowly looked back over one shoulder.

He hadn't turned to face her and there was nothing approachable in his expression or in the quizzical eyebrow he raised when she didn't immediately begin to speak.

She snatched a breath and sent up a prayer, suddenly knowing just how important it was that she found the right words.

'Luke, I am sorry I jumped down your throat,' she said earnestly, her hands knotted together. 'It's just... Oh, I know it sounds like an easy excuse but I'm sure it's the stress of the whole situation getting to me...getting to both of us.'

With a flood of relief she saw him slowly turn to rest one shoulder against the doorway and hurried to continue while he was willing to listen.

'Everything's happened in such a hurry,' she went on. 'You were barely on your feet and out of hospital when you came back to work, then you heard that the in-laws from hell were going to try to take Jenny away. Next, you realised you were going to have to burn the midnight oil to transform your house so that faceless bureaucrats would deem it a suitable place to bring Jenny up, then, on a broad hint from some lawyer, you came up with the idea of this marriage of convenience.' She shrugged. 'No wonder we're so tense.'

She watched him close his eyes and lean his head back against the pristine woodwork and saw how dark the shadows had grown under his eyes. All the time he'd been smiling and talking with their guests today she hadn't really noticed, but now she could see the evidence of how little sleep he must have had over the last couple of weeks. Or was it months?

'You're right,' he murmured, and rubbed one hand over his face in a tired gesture. 'But I owe you an apology, too. If I'd been thinking straight, I would have explained what I'd organised about the sleeping arrangements from the outset, rather than leaving you to guess.'

His eyes opened again and all of a sudden she found herself trapped by the laser-like intensity of his blue gaze.

For several long seconds she almost forgot to breathe as a strange tension sparked in the air between them.

She was totally powerless to break the strange connection and was almost limp with relief when he finally looked away to gaze across at the new sofa-bed.

'Is this going to work?' he asked quietly, a touch of gravel in his voice. 'I'm beginning to wonder if the whole idea was the result of a manic brainstorm brought on by too much work and worry and not enough sleep.'

Cassie's heart took a sudden dive towards her feet. Luke had so many worries that the last thing she wanted was that her presence would add to them. It didn't matter that a purely selfish side of her didn't want to lose the chance of spending this time with him. That pleasure was a secret she didn't have to reveal to anyone.

'It *will* work. It *has* to work, for Jenny's sake,' she said fiercely, ignoring her own wishes and feelings for the moment and concentrating on the most important issue. 'She's your daughter and you're a good father. You have the right to have her living with you.'

'But do I have the right to achieve it at the cost of *your* happiness?' he countered with a mixture of worry and weariness. 'If this situation…living with me…is going to be too uncomfortable for you…'

Living with me…

His evocative words sent a shiver through her even though she knew what he meant.

'We can work it out,' she declared, hoping her voice sounded more confident than she felt even as she fought to dispel the shadowy sensual images conjured up by her imagination. 'After all, it isn't as if we've got to keep the performance up for an audience all the time. When we're here we can relax our guard a little, can't we? Anyway, we're friends, aren't we? That must count for something.'

Luke was silent for so long that she began to wonder if he was going to reply at all.

She'd thought she was beginning to be able to read his expressions but this time, although she could tell that he was busy with his thoughts, she couldn't discern any of them. It was almost as though he was intentionally maintaining a poker face while he deliberated his way to a conclusion.

When he finally spoke there was an air of quiet resignation in his tone.

'As you say, we've been friends for quite a while now, and that *should* count for something. But I still think this agreement goes way beyond the realms of friendship,' he added dryly, shouldering himself away from the doorway. 'Give me a shout if you need some more space. I've emptied some of the drawers and shoved my things up to one end of the wardrobe.'

As he left the nursery and disappeared along the corridor, Cassie was left with the strange impression of things left unsaid...important things...and the feeling that nothing had really been resolved.

'Was that an update from Theatre?' Sahru demanded, pouncing on Cassie as soon as she put the phone down. 'How are Amy and Zoe? How far have they gone with the separation?'

For a second, Cassie nearly snapped at the young

woman and only just managed to bite her tongue in time, knowing how desperate she was for news of the Siamese twins and their big operation. The increasing tension between Luke and herself over the last few days seemed to have doubled her usual misery with PMT, but that wasn't a good enough excuse for giving in to bad temper.

'No news yet, Sahru,' she said, and concentrated briefly on entering into the computer the requisition information she'd just been given over the phone before she glanced up again. 'Anyway, I *did* promise I'd let you know as soon as I heard anything.'

The younger woman grimaced, but even that couldn't mar her stunning good looks. It was no mystery why the number of loitering males had gone up since Sahru had started work in the department. Sometimes it seemed as if every unmarried man on St Augustine's staff had found an excuse to visit...and several of the married ones, too.

Unfortunately, Cassie knew it also meant that, good as Sahru was at the demanding job and much as she seemed to enjoy it, she was unlikely to remain in the specialist unit very long. She would hardly be the first beautiful woman to give up her career for love and marriage.

Although, now that Cassie thought about it, she hadn't noticed that Sahru was particularly eager to take up any of the invitations showered on her. Had Cassie misread the situation? Was her colleague already in a relationship? That certainly wouldn't please her most ardent pursuer, 'Hal' Halawa, the unit's favourite anaesthetist.

'How are you enjoying working in the special care baby unit?' Cassie enquired casually, hoping to find a way to lead in to the question she really wanted to ask. Once they found good staff, the unit was obviously keen to hold onto them.

'I love it,' Sahru declared simply, and the gleam in her

enormous dark eyes underlined her fervour. 'This is all I wanted to do all my life.'

'Until you marry and have babies of your own,' Cassie suggested, playing devil's advocate.

'No.' She shook her head firmly. 'I cannot marry. For me there will be no children, so I will take care of children for others.'

'*Cannot* marry?' Cassie echoed with a frown as she replayed the absolute certainty in the younger woman's tone. 'Do you mean because you can't go outside your own culture? Is it forbidden?'

'Not forbidden. It is my own decision. I have known since I was a young girl that I would not have children. Would not marry.' She spoke quietly in her slightly awkward way, her accent adding an air of mystery to the words.

'That doesn't necessarily follow,' Cassie pointed out. 'Even if you can't have children, that doesn't have to stop you getting married. You must have noticed that Hal has been casting sheep's eyes in your direction ever since you started work here.'

Sahru looked startled. 'When has he been throwing the eyes of sheep?' she demanded. 'Where does he throw them?'

Cassie bit her tongue but couldn't stop a chuckle escaping.

'I'm sorry, Sahru. I'm not laughing at you. It's just that I hadn't realised just how silly that English expression is,' she apologised. 'It just means that Hal can't keep his eyes away from you whenever he comes here. I'm sure he's halfway in love with you already. Doesn't he come from your part of the world?'

'He is from Egypt and I am from Sudan. Our countries are side by side and both of us lived close to the River

Nile when we were children,' she said, clearly unaware that her softened expression was so revealing.

Cassie hid a smile.

It was obvious that, for all Sahru's protestations, she and the handsome young anaesthetist must have spoken at least long enough to have discovered this shared background. The hint of colour darkening the clean crests of her cheekbones clearly hinted at a greater attraction than the young woman was willing to admit.

'Well, it sounds as though you have lots in common. There would be no reason why the two of you couldn't spend some time together and get to know each other as friends,' she prompted. 'Hal really is a nice man, apart from being well qualified and with a good job.'

'Yes... I mean, no...' Sahru objected hurriedly, but instead of the coyness Cassie had expected to see, she was almost certain she'd spotted a flash of fear in the young woman's eyes.

'He is a good man but there could be nothing between the two of us,' she continued with a frantic spate of words. 'He is a doctor and has a good family. Father and mother and a younger sister. I have nothing and no one and...it is not possible for there to be any...anything between us. It is absolutely not possible.'

Before Cassie could say any more Sahru had hurried away, her normally elegant walk transformed into an awkward stumbling rush.

'Damn,' Cassie muttered under her breath. She'd wanted to get to know her new colleague a bit better and had wanted to encourage her to allow friendship into her life even if it didn't lead to marriage, but had only ended up upsetting her.

And it was still several hours before she could curl up in her bed with a hot-water bottle to relieve the horribly familiar ache that was building up in the depths of her pelvis and across her back.

Sometimes the severity of her symptoms made her contemplate that it might even be worth getting pregnant just for the guarantee of nine months without this misery.

Unfortunately, she'd only found one man she would like to be the father of any child she carried, and while she might be married to him at the moment he didn't love her and their marriage wasn't a situation she could count on for the long term. Once his precious Jennywren had been returned to her rightful place with him, Cassie would become superfluous to requirements. It would just be a matter of time before she found herself excluded from their lives.

Admittedly, the week since their marriage hadn't all been plain sailing. It had had its high spots, such as the ritual kiss he bestowed on her each day in front of their colleagues before they went their separate ways and the companionable arm he slung around her waist or shoulders if they happened to meet in the staffroom.

Unfortunately, this camaraderie seemed to be confined to the times when they were in company. At other times there was an uncomfortable edge to their conversation and she'd noticed that they both seemed to be going out of their way to avoid spending their off-duty time together.

On her part, she was torn between wanting to spend every possible moment with the man she loved and fear that doing so would increase the chances for him to discover that love.

She didn't dare look further into the future than the next few days. Just the thought of life without Luke in it was enough to deepen the ache inside her. And that pain had nothing to do with the time of the month.

The phone rang again and she deliberately blocked this

morning's Technicolor memory of Luke on his way out of the bathroom, refusing to dwell on the image his damp tousled hair and sleepy eyes.

Her own eyes had briefly disobeyed her brain to take in a lightning inventory of the rest of his body and had realised that he'd been wearing nothing more than a towel twisted around his waist. She'd caught her first glimpse of an angry red scar snaking its way down his thigh before she'd torn her eyes away and hurried to shut the door between them.

'Special Care Baby Unit. Cassie Mills speaking,' she said, answering by rote when she picked the phone up.

'Cassie *Thornton*,' corrected a teasing voice, and her mental image of Luke's half-naked body flooded back with a vengeance.

'Luke,' she breathed, and her heart performed several impossible somersaults before she got it under control again. 'How can I help? Is there news about Amy and Zoe?'

'Separation is complete,' he announced with a satisfied tone to his voice. 'They're on separate tables now, for the final stages, then they'll come straight down to you.'

'How is Zoe?' she demanded quietly, knowing it was the weaker twin's rapidly worsening condition which had forced the operation to be performed so soon. She knew that Luke had been seriously concerned that both babies' lives might be in jeopardy if the situation continued too long. At least, once they were separated, Amy stood a good chance of surviving even if her twin didn't.

'She's very fragile,' he admitted grimly, 'but the operation went far more smoothly than anticipated, and far faster. Hopefully, that will mean that they'll both recover from the trauma that much quicker. Then all we have to do is keep them stable while their livers grow.'

'Shall I send my nurses up yet?' Sahru wasn't the only one champing at the bit. Karen, too, was waiting to accompany her little charge.

Even though the two of them could now be placed in separate beds for the first time in their lives, experience had shown that Siamese twins would recover better if their 'other half' remained as close as possible. Still, they were both so small that there was going to be plenty of room for them to lie side by side in the same cot, even with all the equipment they would need.

Luke chuckled. 'If your nurses are anything like you, I bet they can't wait to get up here and see what's going on.'

'Guilty, as charged,' Cassie admitted with an answering laugh. 'In fact, given half a chance, you'd probably have the whole department up there, waiting.'

The smile lingered even after she'd put the phone down. It had been so nice to hold a conversation without having to watch every word, the way they seemed to do when they met face to face.

'Well?' demanded Karen, and Cassie jumped. 'What's the news? Are they all right?'

'Is the operation over? Can we go up yet?' Sahru joined in.

'Oh, for heaven's sake. You may as well. Neither of you is worth the space you take up while you're hopping up and down like that,' she chided in exasperation. 'The major part of the operation is over and they're working on them separately now to finish off.'

Sahru's beaming smile made words unnecessary as the two of them narrowly avoided running pell-mell out of the unit.

A high-pitched warning sound drew her eyes towards their most recent arrival, and her feet were moving almost before she realised as she saw the spasmodic movements that told her another seizure was in progress.

Simon Thrush was a very sick baby and they'd all realised, as soon as they'd known the diagnosis, that no matter what they did he was unlikely to survive.

At first the midwife had just thought that Simon's mother was being ultra-careful not to put on too much weight during the pregnancy. It had been difficult to confirm whether the baby had just been growing unusually slowly in the uterus because the first-time mother had refused to have an ultrasound scan on the grounds that the sonic waves might damage her baby's brain development.

It hadn't been until his premature birth just a few hours ago that the full extent of Simon's problem had been revealed.

Pamina had reset the alarm by the time Cassie reached her side, and they looked down at the struggling infant bathed in the unearthly blue glow of the bilirubin light.

In a unit full of tiny babies and with the camouflage of the mask protecting his eyes it wasn't immediately obvious that Simon's head was much smaller than normal, but the signs of his jaundice were growing clearer with every hour. His skin was becoming increasingly yellow in spite of the treatment with the special lights positioned over his cot.

'At first just his head was jaundiced, but it's already reached his chest and arms,' Pamina murmured unhappily as she checked each of the monitor leads and the various IV lines delivering fluids and medication to make sure none had been dislodged by the seizure.

Cassie cast an eye over Simon's chart but there was nothing there to relieve the gloom.

As soon as he'd arrived on the unit he'd had a whole

battery of tests, including X-rays of his head and analysis of his cerebrospinal fluid.

They were still trying to stabilise him when the awful diagnosis had been made.

'Congenital toxoplasmosis?' Celia Thrush had repeated in disbelief when Cassie had taken her into the little interview room for Luke to speak to her. 'But there aren't any congenital illnesses in our family, and we don't use any genetically modified food or chemicals so it can't be that.'

'It's caused by an infection during pregnancy,' Luke had explained gently. 'Sometimes it can be caught by eating undercooked meat, but the most common cause is cats.'

'I've got cats. Five of them,' she admitted, 'but they certainly haven't got any infections. We live right out of town and they never see any other cats to catch anything.'

'Are they wormed regularly with a product that will clear them of Toxoplasma gondii?'

'They don't *need* worming,' she snapped. 'I *told* you, they never see any other cats to pick up any infections. Anyway, I don't believe in dosing everything with all these chemicals and injections. Everybody knows that you doctors hand out too many unnecessary prescriptions, and vets are probably the same.'

Cassie held her breath but Luke wisely refrained from responding to the woman's belligerent tone. It was common enough for the parents of their little patients to lash out at staff when fear for their child took over.

'Oh, God, I'm sorry,' Celia Thrush, murmured distractedly into the uncomfortable silence. 'I'm just so... I wasn't expecting him to arrive so soon. Is he very sick? How long will it take before he's strong enough for me to take him home?'

'Mrs Thrush, Simon *is* very sick. You were probably infected with the *Toxoplasma gondii* organism when you came into contact with cat faeces and the infection passed to him while he was growing inside you.'

'What's wrong with him? What has the bug done to him and what can you do about it?' There was an air of desperation in her voice and Cassie thought that the poor woman had probably begun to guess what Luke's answer was going to be.

'He's got jaundice—that's why his skin looks so yellow, and it's why we've got the special lights shining on his skin. He's also suffering from inflammation of his eyes and his heart, enlargement of his liver and spleen and high spinal-fluid pressure from increased fluid around the brain. The X-rays showed that there's also evidence of calcium deposits in his brain and he's been having seizures.'

Tears were silently trickling down the young woman's cheeks by the time Luke finished his litany of disaster and Cassie had to swallow hard to stop herself crying, too.

'We're treating the infection with a combination of antiparasitic and antibacterial drugs and he's having corticosteriods for the inflammation, but...' He paused, as though searching for the kindest way to say the dreadful words.

'He's going to die, isn't he?' Celia whispered hoarsely, her pale blue eyes swimming in an ocean of despair. 'My baby's going to die.'

Knowing that the child had already suffered permanent damage to his heart, brain and eyes and that he would very likely be deaf and suffer increasing seizures, that didn't lessen Cassie's sympathy for the mother who was about to lose him. There was always a very narrow line between wanting what was best for the grieving parent and what was best for the suffering baby.

'I'm sorry, Mrs Thrush,' Luke said.

He didn't need to say any more. They all understood that there was little chance of Simon surviving many days in his worsening condition, and no chance at all of him ever living a healthy life.

For several seconds the young woman's eyes travelled wildly from Luke to Cassie and back again before she burst into racking sobs.

'It's my fault, isn't it?' she wailed, almost incoherent in her grief. 'My baby's dying and it's all my fault.'

Silently Cassie wrapped a comforting arm around the shuddering shoulders, nodding her thanks as Luke passed her a box of paper hankies as he quietly left the room.

'Cassie? Are you there?'

The soft voice drew Cassie out of an uneasy doze and she groaned as she turned to face its source, dimly outlined in the doorway.

'Luke?' she murmured, surprised to see how dark it had become. 'I only intended curling up for a little while. I must have fallen asleep.'

She suddenly realised that she was lying in the middle of Luke's bed and was grateful for the dim light seeping in from the landing when she felt the surge of heat rise in her cheeks.

The couch in the sitting room was too lumpy and uncomfortable for lying down and she hadn't been able to face dragging her own bed out when she'd arrived home with her stomach aching worse than ever. The sight of Luke's neatly made bed had been irresistible and she'd curled up with the hot-water bottle cradled against her stomach and waited for relief.

If she hadn't given in to tears over little Simon Thrush's death she probably wouldn't have fallen asleep. Then she would have been able to straighten the covers on Luke's bed before he arrived home and he'd have been none the wiser. As it was, she'd been caught red-handed.

Feeling strangely vulnerable, she scrambled to sit up, but when she went to swing her feet to the floor the hot-water bottle fell with an easily recognisable thud.

'What was that?' Luke's words were accompanied by a click and a sudden flood of light as he switched on the lamp beside the bed.

Cassie cringed as he looked from her to the bottle. She was all too easily able to guess what a mess she looked and could only hope that he would think her heavy-eyed look was the result of her sleep and not the bout of tears.

She certainly wouldn't be looking as sexily sleepy as Luke had this morning on his way out of the bathroom.

'Backache or...?' he asked cryptically.

'Or,' she said with a grimace to hide her embarrassment. He was a doctor and her husband but that didn't make her any more comfortable with the topic. Kirstin and Naomi knew about her problems but she wasn't in the habit of discussing them with anyone else.

'Are you feeling any easier now?' he asked as he bent to retrieve the bottle, obviously guessing what she'd been using it for. 'This is cold. Do you want me to refill it?'

She was going to insist on taking care of it herself but the idea of trailing all the way down to the kitchen to heat some water when he was willing to was too much.

'Yes, please,' she agreed. 'It isn't often as bad as this, but at least it doesn't usually last for long. Then I've got a whole four weeks before I go through it again, thank goodness.'

'Have you eaten anything since you came home?' he

asked, pausing in the doorway. 'How about taking some painkillers?'

'I couldn't face cooking anything, and the thought of pulling the settee out and making up my bed...' She gestured towards her huddled position on the side of his generous double bed. 'I'd better get that done now.'

'Leave it,' he directed, and waggled the noisy hot-water bottle. 'I'll go and fill this and sort your bed out when I come back up with it. You can lie down and curl up until I've got everything organised.'

He didn't wait for her to reply and she was glad he'd gone when she felt a stray tear slide down her cheek.

They'd been tiptoeing around each other for days, almost as if they'd never been friends, but as soon as he'd realised that she was in pain he'd reverted to the kind, thoughtful friend he'd always been. After the overload of emotion she always suffered when the unit lost one of their charges his empathy was almost enough to set the tears off again.

She buried her face in his pillow and breathed deeply, all too aware of the mixture of soap and man surrounding her.

She had to stifle a sob when she realised that, although the two of them had been married for a week, this was the first time she'd ever lain on his bed.

Even now, she was lying on it alone and she was beginning to wonder if there would ever come a time when she would share a bed with the man she loved. She certainly didn't want to share one with anyone else and she was getting so tired of having to pretend that Luke was nothing more than her friend.

This certainly wasn't the sort of relationship that Naomi was looking forward to with Edward Sullivan, and that fact had made her conversations with her friend very difficult. Naomi wanted to indulge in girl talk now that her own wedding was coming closer while Cassie herself was shying away. How could she pretend to give advice when she knew nothing more now than she had two years ago?

If things had been different… If Luke had realised that he'd been in love with her all along… If their marriage had happened for all the right reasons… If—

'Cassie?'

As if her thoughts had conjured him up she could hear his voice. Gentle. Caring.

She had dreamed for a long time that one day they would lie together with his arms wrapped around her, their bodies fitting together as perfectly as two spoons.

She would be able to feel his warmth against her, his strong hands soothing her aches while his breath bathed the side of her face and the steady beat of his heart lulled her to sleep as effortlessly as a lullaby.

Cassie surfaced slowly.

Something was different but she was too dozy to try to work out what it was. All she knew was that she'd never felt so deliciously warm and comfortable in her life.

It almost felt as if she had her arm wrapped around an enormous cuddly bear, but instead of a thick furry pelt he had silky hairs that tickled her nose. He was very warm, too, with a rhythmic beat in his chest that almost made it seem as if he were alive.

'Cassie,' the bear said in a deep husky rumble, and she had to smile. His voice was just perfect. Almost a growl, but not quite. And as for the rest of him…

Drifting in a world that was half dream, half fantasy, she began to explore. She had only got as far as discovering one tight male nipple when her investigations were brought to a sudden halt by a large paw that wasn't a paw.

'Cassie, open your eyes,' demanded the husky voice and she reluctantly obeyed, lifting heavy lids to find herself looking straight into Luke's intent blue gaze.

'Luke,' she breathed with a smile.

Her fantasies had never been this real before, even in the days before she'd forbidden herself to think about him as anything other than a friend.

Back then she'd often tried to imagine what it would be like to find herself wrapped in his arms with his gaze fixed on her lips as though the one thing he wanted most in all the world was to taste them.

'Kiss me,' she whispered as she slid her fingers up to tangle in the thickness of his hair, hoping desperately that the dream wouldn't fade before she felt his lips meet hers. 'Please, Luke, kiss me.'

CHAPTER NINE

'CASSIE,' Luke groaned just before her name was lost in an avalanche of sensation.

In an instant Cassie knew that this was no dream, but when she felt Luke's lips meet hers it ceased to matter. Nothing mattered as long as she could hold him and feel the lean length of his body against hers, feel the furious beat of his heart and the urgency of his touch.

This was everything she'd always dreamed, only more…and better.

The naked skin of his shoulders was every bit as smooth as it looked, but so much warmer, as was the lean muscular length of his back. His hands were just as agile and adept as they were when he slid a needle into a vein no thicker than a piece of sewing cotton, but so much more arousing when they slid up over her ribs to cradle her breasts.

One powerful thigh nudged her legs apart as he lowered his weight onto the cradle of her hips and she couldn't help but be aware of how aroused he was, too.

Suddenly he froze, every muscle locked solid, and she couldn't suppress a whimper of disappointment.

Questions tumbled through her head.

Why had he stopped? Had she done something wrong? Had he suddenly remembered that she was Cassie and not—?

'Dammit!' he cursed as he flung the tumbled bed-clothes aside and leapt off the bed. 'Cassie, I'm sorry…'

Stunned by his abrupt departure, she had a brief eye-catching view of his very aroused body clothed only in a pair of underpants before he turned his back on her and tried to force one foot into his disreputable jeans.

Before she could find the words to demand an explanation she heard the strident sound of the front doorbell.

'Who the blazes is that, coming round at such an ungodly hour?' Luke demanded as he grabbed a paint-stained sweatshirt and dragged it over his head. 'It had better not be a door-to-door salesman or I'll tell him what I think of him,' he continued as he stormed out of the room, apparently oblivious of the fact that his feet were still bare and the button at his waistband gaped tantalisingly.

Cassie glanced across at his alarm clock as she listened to his footsteps pounding heavily down the stairs, and stared.

'It's nearly ten o'clock,' she gasped, panic-stricken for a moment that she might be late for her shift, then flopped back onto the pillow when she remembered that she was on late duty today.

In the background she could hear voices but it wasn't until she heard the renewed sound of feet on the stairs that she realised that Luke was on his way back—in a hurry!

There was barely time for her to realise that she was still lying in the bed she'd somehow ended up sharing with him last night when he burst into the bedroom.

'Cassie, get up!' he ordered in a hoarse whisper, his cheeks flushed as though with embarrassment as he pushed the door closed behind him. 'Quickly! It's the social worker person. I think she's come to check up on the house…to see if it's safe for Jenny.'

'What? You mean now?' She shot up in the bed and suddenly realised that her only covering appeared to be a pair of panties and one of Luke's T-shirts. When had she put that on—or had he? It was twisted up almost as far as her armpits.

The memory of how it had ended up there heated her cheeks enough for spontaneous combustion and she scrambled to regain her dignity while she pulled it down to a more modest level.

'You take the bathroom,' he suggested as he dragged hasty fingers through his endearingly tousled hair. 'I'll go down and put some coffee on or something, then we can swap over.' He turned to hurry away.

'Luke,' she called softly, torn between nervousness at the importance of this meeting and the urge to laugh at cool, competent Luke's unaccustomed agitation.

'What?' He paused in the doorway and Cassie thought he had never looked more vulnerable or more appealing.

'You might want to think about fastening your jeans before you go back down,' she suggested with a straight face. 'That dreadful sweatshirt's covered in paint and your cleanest trainers are over there, by the wardrobe.'

He glanced down at his gaping fly and naked feet and she heard him swear softly under his breath as colour washed up into his face again.

This time she couldn't control a wicked chuckle and when his head whipped towards her to deliver an affronted glare she laughed even harder.

'So you think this is funny, do you?' he demanded as he advanced on her with a fiendish gleam in his eye. 'I didn't notice *you* scrambling to drag some clothes on to answer the door. Perhaps I should send you down to meet the woman just as you are and see how *you* like it.'

'No!' Cassie squeaked as she scrambled for the other side of the bed. She lost her hold on the bedspread she'd been clutching against herself, and when she felt sinewy fingers fasten around her ankle and start to drag her remorselessly towards him across the mattress she completely forgot that there was a stranger in the house.

'Don't you dare tickle me,' she warned, feeling the helpless laughter coming closer the nearer his outstretched fingers came to her ribs. 'Please, Luke, don't...don't...!'

He barely touched her but it was more than enough to have her giggling helplessly while she squirmed and wriggled in a hopeless attempt at evasion.

She was limp and breathless by the time he stopped and totally shocked when she heard a knock and a strange voice just outside the bedroom door.

'Excuse me. Is everything all right in there?'

Luke froze and when Cassie saw the petrified expression on his face it nearly set her off again and she had to grab a pillow to stifle her mirth.

'Dr Thornton?' the voice called again.

'Uh, yes. Yes, everything's fine,' he said in confusion as he shot off the bed and hastily scrabbled about for his trainers, one hand fumbling with the button at his waistband.

Cassie slid off the thoroughly scrambled bed and grabbed Luke's dressing-gown. She'd barely thrust her hands down the sleeves when there was another tentative knock at the door.

'Coming,' she called in a voice that wasn't quite as steady as she would have liked. Still, the only solution to the embarrassing situation she could think of at short notice was to brazen it out.

'Look, I'm awfully sorry we aren't up and about this morning,' she gabbled as she pulled the door open and produced her friendliest smile.

The woman looked to be about her own age but was dressed quietly and elegantly in a smart navy suit with not a hair out of place. Cassie could only guess what *she* looked like after her tussle with Luke and wearing his enormous dressing-gown, and didn't dare to meet the woman's eyes. She would have loved to have raked her fingers through her hair to get it off her face but was afraid that would only draw attention to it.

She ventured a quick glance in Luke's direction when a hastily flung tatty sweatshirt caught her eye. The rustling sounds told her he was donning a fresh shirt but couldn't begin to tell her that he looked like a manic cartoon character while he was trying to do it.

'You see, Luke had a late night at the hospital last night and I'm not due at work until one this afternoon so...so we had a bit of a lie-in.'

Cassie only needed a glimpse of the expression on the woman's face to know what she thought had been going on in the bedroom before she'd interrupted. It was exactly what *she* would have liked to have gone on, had the circumstances been different. But she didn't have time to think about that now.

'Unfortunately, I've got some very ticklish spots and Luke seems to know exactly how to find them...' she continued, aghast at what she could hear herself revealing but desperate to fill the uncomfortable silence while they waited for Luke to appear.

'You don't have to tell her *all* our secrets, my love,' he chided as he joined her in the doorway and slid his arm familiarly around her waist.

The casual endearment startled her into silence while his nonchalant action reactivated all the vibrating nerves she'd been trying so hard to subdue. The sensory overload flooding through her at his closeness almost stopped her from hearing the end of his conversation.

As it was, she had to drag her infatuated concentration

back when he spoke directly to her, swiftly reminding herself that it was all a game of make-believe especially for the woman in front of them.

'Why don't you grab the bathroom while I put the kettle on?' he suggested with an apparently loving squeeze that sent her pulse rate up several notches in spite of her stern reminder. 'What would everyone prefer? Tea or coffee?'

'Cassie, I'm sorry,' he'd said as he'd leapt out of bed and her badly bruised ego wouldn't let her banish the words out of her head.

Why had he been sorry? Had it been just because they'd been interrupted, or had it been because they never should have started in the first place?

The frustrating thing was that, as the day went on, she was forced to admit that the reason she didn't dare ask him was because she was afraid to find out the answer.

'Fearless Cassie Mills isn't so fearless any more,' she muttered wryly as she leant back against the work surface in the tiny staff kitchen. Furiously, she scraped out the last of her yoghurt, cross that he had so effortlessly put such a large chink in her armour. 'In fact, she isn't even Cassie *Mills* any more.'

It seemed as if with her change of name had come a radical change in personality. The unwanted child who had grown into a scrappy teenager willing to take on the world to achieve her goals had apparently disappeared overnight.

All Luke had to do was touch her and—

'Cassie, I just spoke to that lawyer chap,' Luke said as she leant across to throw away the plastic pot, his voice coming out of the blue as if her thoughts had conjured him up and almost sending her into orbit.

She whirled to face him and was just in time to be whisked off her feet and spun in a giddy circle.

'Wh-what?' she stammered as her feet touched the floor again, but her knees were far too wobbly to hold her. She had a feeling that it was Luke's proximity and his broad grin which were to blame rather than another exuberant twirl.

'You know I phoned him as soon as Mrs Gosling left the house this morning. Well, he's just got back to me.'

'So soon?' Cassie exclaimed. 'I thought it would take days or even weeks before we heard anything.'

'It may well take that long before we get all the paperwork through, but he managed to speak to her just as she returned to her office.'

'And?' she prompted, her spirits lifting like a helium-filled balloon. She knew from his smug expression that it must be good news.

'And she was absolutely delighted with the house, especially Jennywren's room. Furthermore, she thought we were a delightful couple and there was obviously no truth to the Paynes' accusation that ours was a sham marriage.'

Luke was obviously so delighted with the report that Cassie almost managed to ignore the sudden stab of guilt at the reminder.

Unfortunately, she could still hear the echo of Dot's voice over the years as she'd tried to impress on them that two wrongs didn't make a right.

That maxim was all too easily translated into the present situation.

The fact that the Paynes were trying to take Jenny away from the father who loved her was undoubtedly wrong. It wasn't enough that it would lessen their own sadness and loss. But the same thing could be said about the pretence of the marriage she and Luke had entered into. It had been done for the best of motives, but they were still living a lie.

'Oh, Cassie,' Luke murmured as he wrapped both arms around her again and gave her a heartfelt hug. 'He said it could be just a matter of days before he can prod the system into letting Jenny come home with us.'

'What? Permanently? Just like that?' Cassie was stunned. Going by the cases she'd seen on television she'd thought that their time together might stretch into months and even years before everything was resolved. Was she going to lose Luke after only a couple of weeks?

'I wish!' he exclaimed fervently. 'No. It will probably be just for a visit the first time, until the legal eagles can cross all the t's and dot the i's. Perhaps just an afternoon or maybe even a whole weekend if I'm lucky. But at least it will give the two of us time to get to know each other again.'

Remembering the beaming smile and the way Jenny had reached for her father that day at the Paynes' house, Cassie didn't think that would take long. In spite of the traumatic loss of her mother and the intervening weeks spent with her grandparents while Luke had been in hospital, it was obvious that the child hadn't forgotten her father at all.

The thing that made her heart ache was the way he'd been speaking about the two of them, himself and Jenny, getting to know each other. It was as if, because her presence in their lives was only intended to be temporary, she had no importance in the overall scheme of things.

'I'm pleased for you,' she said honestly as she reached for a cloth to wipe down the draining-board to occupy her hands. How could she not be glad with this evidence of progress when it was the whole point of their secret collaboration? 'Let me know as soon as you're given a date. I'll need to know what you want me to do about my shifts.'

'What do you mean, what I want you to do?' he asked warily, as if he'd just realised she wasn't quite as ecstatic about his news as he was.

'Well, I need to know in case you'd rather spend the time with her by yourself,' she managed coolly, in spite of the ache inside her. She'd already lost her heart to the lovable child, completely captivated by her cheerful exuberance and the spontaneous hugs she'd received.

'Don't be silly. Why would I want to shut you out?' he began with a puzzled frown. Then it disappeared as his face suddenly went blank and unreadable as other implications dawned on him. 'Unless you'd rather not spend time with us?'

'That's up to you. I wouldn't want to intrude...' she said, still polishing the stainless steel as though her life depended on it.

'Oh, for heaven's sake!' he muttered impatiently. 'I thought you liked Jenny. You certainly seemed to get on with her when you took over her bathtime—or was that pretence, too?'

'No, it *wasn't* pretence,' she insisted, stung into facing him. 'She's an absolute sweetheart and I loved every minute of it. I just didn't want you to think I was presuming...'

'Cassie? Hush a minute.' He stilled the hands that were wringing the cloth between them into a tight rope and threw it into the sink. 'I have absolutely no intention of excluding you from any arrangements. Jenny's visits will be something we share between us.'

The way his blue eyes were staring so intently into hers was doing strange things to her pulse and breathing, and for a moment she almost felt as if she could happily drown in their depths.

As ever, when confronted by unmanageable emotions she retreated to hide behind humour.

'Does that mean we *both* get to change her nappies and get soaking wet at bathtime?'

'Of course. Unless you want to fight me for the honour?' His eyes gleamed as he threw her a wicked grin and her heart somersaulted wildly before she managed to force it to behave.

'No chance!' she exclaimed with an answering grin. 'You'd let me win and then try to tell me you were just being gentlemanly!'

'Well, we can certainly tell that you two are married by the way you're arguing!' said a familiar voice as Naomi propped herself in the doorway. 'Is this what I've got to look forward to?'

'If you're lucky,' Luke retorted with a sexy wink at Cassie. 'It's the making up afterwards that's the fun, isn't it?'

'If you say so, dear,' Cassie replied with her best impression of a downtrodden wife which fooled no one.

'Were you looking for me, Naomi?' Luke asked through his laughter.

'Yes and no.' She frowned fiercely at both of them. 'The two of you do realise that you've thrown all my months of careful planning out of the window?'

'What planning? How?' Luke was obviously confused but Cassie could guess what Naomi was talking about. Her perfect wedding was becoming her sole topic of conversation the closer the date drew.

'Well, ever since we were teenagers we've planned that whichever of us got married first would have the other two as bridesmaids,' Naomi explained for Luke's benefit.

'And?'

'And when I started planning mine I went to a lot of trouble to find out what sort of dresses Cassie and Kirstin wanted to wear...'

'More like what sort of dresses we refused to be seen dead in,' Cassie butted in slyly.

'And then,' Naomi continued, ignoring Cassie and directing her complaint at Luke, 'when the decision was finally made and the dressmaker got started on them, you and Cassie got married.'

'So?' Luke still didn't understand what the problem was if his puzzled expression was anything to go by.

'So, Cassie isn't a brides*maid* any more, is she? She's married, so she has to be matron of honour.'

Cassie saw the instant that Luke's wicked sense of humour caught hold of the idea that she would now be considered a matron and hurried to head him off before he said anything to upset her friend. Not that he'd do it on purpose, but he didn't know much it mattered to Naomi that everything was absolutely perfect on her big day.

'Don't worry about it, Naomi,' she soothed quickly. 'I'd far rather be a matron of honour in a bridesmaid's dress to match Kirstin than have to wear something different. It will look much better on the photos if we're dressed the same, too.'

She'd obviously hit the right note because it was a much happier Naomi who departed a few minutes later, leaving Cassie and Luke to return to work.

Luke had obviously been thinking overnight about their conversation with Naomi because he brought it up when they were sharing breakfast the next morning.

'Cassie, how much does all that formal wedding stuff really matter?' he asked thoughtfully, surprising her as she retrieved the first two slices of toast and put another two in the toaster.

His elbows were planted on the table with his first mug of strong black coffee cradled between both hands, the steam rising sinuously across his thoughtful expression.

'What do you mean? To me, or to people in general?'

'Both, I suppose. I can remember Mrs Payne making terse comments about having to throw everything together in a hurry if the baby wasn't to arrive before we'd made it legal. Sophie was upset, too, that we couldn't have the reception in the big hotel where she wanted it because they were booked up at least a year ahead.'

'I don't know about Sophie and her mother, but sometimes the big flashy wedding is just a matter of blatant snobbery. On the other hand, to some people it matters a lot, especially to someone like Naomi who's spent most of her life craving a family of her own. She's been looking forward for years to having all the trimmings that everyone else takes for granted so that she'll finally feel that she fits in.'

'What about you?' he asked quietly. 'What sort of marriage did you have in mind when you were growing up? Did I cheat you out of your big day by coercing you into this arrangement?'

'Not at all,' she said lightly while her thoughts whirled at a million miles an hour, trying to find a safe path through the minefield ahead.

She could hardly tell him that the only person she'd ever woven fancy daydreams around had been Dr Luke Thornton. That she'd fallen for him almost the first time they'd met and that when he'd married Sophie he'd broken her heart.

She certainly couldn't tell him that her secret daydreams now revolved around that same Dr Luke Thornton suddenly discovering that he was madly in love with her.

And he wanted to know what sort of marriage she dreamed about? She didn't dare touch that with a barge-pole.

'I've always felt that it was the marriage that mattered more than the wedding. That if the man I was marrying was the one and only man for me and he felt the same way, then it wouldn't matter to either of us how grand or how simple the ceremony was.'

She held her breath while she deposited toast, butter and marmalade on the table in front of him, expecting at any minute that he'd take the conversation further. Would he apply her words to their own wedding and realise just how revealing they had been or would he dismiss them as hypothetical?

When he stayed lost in thought she breathed a silent sigh of relief, took her chance to grab her own toast and coffee and fled upstairs.

'I thought this whole situation would turn out rather as if the two of us were house-sharing, but it's much more difficult than that,' she muttered as she went through the routine of folding her bed away. 'I didn't count on finding Luke so attractive, neither did I expect to find myself daydreaming about for ever.'

It wasn't as if Luke had given her any reason to believe that he was thinking along the same lines, in spite of the fact that he was facing the prospect of single fatherhood without her.

Was there enough of a bond between the two of them to form the basis of a longer-term relationship? Was it worth exploring?

Luke and Jenny were definitely worth having in her

life, even if they were only nominally hers and only for a short time. But for ever?

Suddenly she found herself sitting heavily on the edge of the sofa-bed and doing some careful thinking. There were a number of ideas she'd been clinging to ever since she'd first understood that neither of her parents had wanted her. It seemed that the time had definitely arrived for her to re-examine them.

She'd already admitted, right from the moment that she'd been making her vows, that she was as much in love with Luke as ever. It hadn't taken much more than a wide smile from his precious Jenny for Luke's daughter to captivate her, too. She would be an easy child to love.

'So why am I making such a song and dance about everything?' she murmured. 'If I love him so much, why haven't I told him? Why am I still sleeping in this bed each night when where I really want to be is in his bed with him?'

The twin spectres of Luke's beautiful first wife and her own disastrous family history rose up the way they always did to taunt her with good solid reasons why she shouldn't take the risk.

'But if I don't take a chance with Luke, will I be glad I didn't set myself up for heartache or will I always wonder what might have been?' she mused aloud, desperately missing being able to talk to Naomi and Kirstin.

'Cassie?'

The sound of Luke's voice breaking into her thoughts was a shock, especially when she realised that he was standing in the open doorway of Jenny's room.

How long had he been standing there?

She had no idea. Neither could she remember how much of her deliberations had been voiced aloud.

How much had he heard? What was he thinking?

CHAPTER TEN

'YOU'RE not going to splash Daddy, are you, my little Jennywren?' Luke said warily as Cassie stood well out of range on the other side of the bathroom. Seeing the amount of water already gleaming on the floor, she was glad that she'd suggested they put the baby bath inside the adult one.

He was kneeling on the wet floor beside the bath with one hand protectively curved around Jenny's shoulders as he rinsed the soap bubbles off her little body.

The sleeves of his rugby shirt were pushed well above his elbows but she could see that they were already thoroughly wet, as was a broad band across his waist where he leant over the edge of the bath.

His cherubic daughter smiled up at him, showing the latest addition to her row of newly emerged teeth, then chattered several unintelligible words. She was the perfect picture of innocence until she brought both hands down onto the frothy surface of the water with a resounding smack and a squeal of delight.

Luke was completely drenched by the resulting tidal wave and when Cassie saw the startled expression on his face she couldn't help laughing out loud.

He turned and glowered at her over his shoulder but that only made it worse. His hair was plastered to his head with rivulets of water trickling down his face and into his open collar. He looked so wet it was almost as if he'd stepped under a shower fully clothed.

'Go ahead and laugh but, just remember, this is *your*

job next time,' he reminded her as he fished a wriggling Jenny out of the water.

'That's no problem,' Cassie said airily as she wrapped a warm towel round the solid little body and blew a raspberry on the side of her wet neck. 'You'll be a good girl for me, won't, you sweetheart?'

'Huh! I wouldn't count on it. I'm going to enjoy seeing you get your comeuppance,' Luke said darkly as he straightened up and stood dripping on the sodden mat.

Cassie was grinning as he squelched his way out of the room, only realising after he'd gone that his obvious move would have been to strip his wet clothes off straight away rather than trail into his bedroom. *That* would have been something worth watching.

But, then, she always thought Luke was worth watching, whether he was concentrating on one of their little patients in the unit or turning out a pair of perfectly fluffy omelettes the way he had last night for their supper.

He was especially attractive to her when she watched him taking care of his precious Jennywren, and it was that side of his character that was drawing her closer and closer to making an irreversible decision.

Ever since he'd come across her musing aloud about for ever there had been an extra air of tension between them when they'd been alone. Cassie knew that they were going to have to talk about it eventually but in the meantime it felt almost like waiting for the other shoe to drop, especially when it seemed as if Luke was just biding his time.

She was hoping that when the conversation finally took place she would have found some much-needed courage. She longed to suggest that, for Jenny's sake if nothing else, she and Luke could try to make a go of a real marriage.

Every time she envisioned such a discussion she felt as if she were being torn in two. One half was still desperately afraid that history would repeat itself, that the marriage would end, leaving her with a broken heart.

Apart from Dot and Arthur, she'd never seen how a successful marriage worked, and Arthur had been taken ill so soon after her arrival that all she really remembered clearly was the heartache and despair Dot had suffered while she'd watched his desperate fight against the cancer destroying him from the inside.

Her own parents certainly hadn't set a pattern she wanted to follow and the rest of the children she'd come to know, albeit briefly before she was moved on, seemed to have similar stories of neglect, abandonment and even abuse.

But there was the other side of her mind, the side ruled by her heart. That was telling her that it was worth risking the embarrassment and pain of a refusal if there was the possibility of an acceptance, the possibility that Luke would agree to change their marriage of convenience to a promise of for ever.

While her emotions were see-sawing over her personal life, her heartstrings were also being tugged at work.

The most recent tragedy they'd seen in the unit had been a baby born to a young girl in the early hours of the morning.

The couple were teenage refugees from a war-torn region in Eastern Europe who'd been airlifted to safety until such time as the situation in their country improved. Each had witnessed the destruction of everything they'd held dear—family, friends and property—and out of such desperation had struck up a friendship which had obviously become much more.

Unused to the health system in their temporarily

adopted country, the first time Ana had been seen by a doctor had been when she's gone into labour and her panic-stricken young partner had flagged down a taxi.

Stefan spoke marginally more English than his terrified companion, but Cassie could understand why Luke had called for the assistance of an interpreter before he'd tried to explain the situation. How could anyone hope to find an easy way to explain that because their baby had been born with most of her brain missing she would be unlikely to live more than a few hours?

'It just isn't fair, is it?' Melissa said, blinking suspiciously bright eyes when the pathetic little body was taken away from the department after her futile two-hour fight for life. 'They've lost everything and everyone, and just when it looks as if they're going to be able to start over—as if something good is going to come out of all that misery...'

Cassie remembered Luke pointing out that no one had promised that life would be fair, and he of all people would know that. From being a happily married man with the start of a family he had ended up in a split second as a widower fighting for his life and the custody of his little daughter.

Cassie wondered if there was a lesson to be learned from all this. Should she take it as a signal that she should seize her own chances while she could?

The high point of the week—Jenny's visit—had taken the two of them completely by surprise and had pushed everything else to the back of Cassie's mind.

Cassie had been sitting quietly, hemming the last of the new curtains for the sitting room while she waited for Luke to take her out grocery shopping, when the phone had rung.

He'd been due home at any minute and she'd half expected to hear his voice warning her that he'd been unavoidably delayed.

'Is Luke there?' demanded an unforgettable voice, and Cassie froze. Why on earth was Mrs Payne phoning?

'H-he's due home any moment,' she stammered, suddenly shaking all over. 'Shall I get him to return your call or do you want me to take a message?'

'Our lawyer suggested that it would be a good idea if we showed willing, so could you tell him that if he wants to take Jennifer home for a visit he can either come to collect her this evening, before ten, or tomorrow morning at eight,' she said briskly.

Cassie was stunned speechless. What on earth had brought about this change of attitude? Did it mean that they would soon be hearing about a date for the court case? Were the Paynes trying to show that they had done their best for Jenny even if it meant allowing her to spend time with her father?

'Of course I'll tell him. Do we need to ring you to let you know when we'll be there?'

'That won't be necessary. Miss Gosling is taking a couple of days off to help her sister to move house and Jennifer is teething. I only need to know if it isn't convenient for you to have her because then I'd have to contact the agency to send someone over.'

'I'm sure it won't be a problem,' Cassie said firmly, suddenly realising that it certainly wasn't the kindness of the Paynes' hearts which had prompted the amazing turnaround but a lack of qualified childcare. 'Whatever happens, there will be one or other of us here to look after Jenny.'

In a split second Cassie decided that she would take some of her holiday entitlement at short notice or even ask for a couple of days off without pay if it came to that. She was determined that nothing should be allowed to interfere with Jenny's first visit.

'As soon as Miss Gosling returns we'll be over to collect Jennifer again,' Luke's in-law from hell continued just as briskly, then paused just long enough for a nasty shiver to travel up Cassie's spine before she went on. 'You'll be earning your money for a couple of days if she's still teething.'

'Earning my money?' Cassie said, puzzled at the strange phrase.

'Oh, come on. You know what I'm talking about,' the older woman said in a scoffing tone. 'The only reason the two of you married in such a hurry was so that he could trick his way into getting custody of the child. I doubt whether you did it without a considerable sum of money passing hands.'

For the second time in as many minutes Cassie was speechless. This time it was a good thing because at least it allowed her to put a leash on her anger—a leash composed partly of guilt because there was a thread of truth in the woman's assertion.

But the idea that she would have accepted money for helping Luke sickened her.

'Are you accusing me of being some sort of prostitute, Mrs Payne? Because if so I have to tell you that I am nothing of the sort nor have I ever been.' She drew in a quivering breath, conscious that she was shaking all over. Was this whole conversation an attempt at rattling her? An excuse to try and trick her into making a damaging confession? The only way Cassie knew to avoid that was to tell nothing less than the truth.

'It's absolutely none of your business,' she continued heatedly, 'but I was a virgin the day I got married and I certainly didn't wait twenty-seven years to sell myself to the highest bidder. I meant every one of the vows I made on my wedding day.'

She ran out of words and narrowly prevented herself from slamming the phone down. Only the thought that Luke was depending on her to help him get Jenny back stayed her hand.

The silence went on for so long that she began to wonder if Mrs Payne had broken the connection instead.

Finally, her voice notably less abrasive than before, the older woman spoke. 'So I take it one of you will be coming over to pick Jennifer up?'

'You can count on it,' Cassie declared firmly. 'We've been looking forward to Jenny coming home.'

With perfunctory farewells on both sides the call ended, and Cassie sank back against the cushions behind her with a shaky sigh and allowed her eyes to close.

'Are you all right?' Luke demanded as he dropped into the seat beside her and nearly scared her to death.

'Oh, Luke, you're home,' she said, and threw herself into his arms with a sob of relief.

'Who on earth was that?' he demanded as he pulled her close and tightened his arms around her till her head rested against his shoulder.

'Mrs Payne,' she announced miserably. 'Oh, Luke, I hope I haven't messed everything up, but when she accused me of taking money from you—'

'Whoa! Cassie! Slow down. What are you talking about? I heard you talking as I came in but I had no idea what it was all about.'

Cassie replayed the conversation in her mind and wondered briefly how much he had overheard. For a moment she wasn't certain whether she wanted Luke to have heard her declaration or not. Although she hadn't actually said the words, she had virtually announced to Mrs Payne that she loved Luke.

Suddenly too nervous to ask, she slipped regretfully out of his arms and hurried to give him the good news, knowing that the prospect of having his beloved Jennywren home would take precedence over any overheard conversation.

Except that the longer the situation went on, the more convinced she became that Luke must have heard more than he'd admitted. Ever since then there had been an electric air about him, as if he was filled with suppressed energy, and it was making her nervous.

It was almost as if there were lightning about, and she had a growing feeling that it was going to strike her at any minute.

For the moment she took refuge in the normality of drying the wriggly little body on her lap and posting little starfish hands into stretchy sleeves.

Jenny was a delight, in spite of the fact that she had two angry patches on her cheeks that warned of the teething misery she was going through.

Luke was pulling a dry rugby shirt on over a noticeably worn pair of jeans when she emerged from the bathroom. Cassie caught a tantalising glimpse of muscles and silky dark body hair and her stomach clenched in reaction.

'Time for bed?' Luke asked, and her heart turned a complete somersault before she reminded it that he was talking about his daughter.

He sat disturbingly close while she cradled the sleepy youngster through the last few mouthfuls of her bottle and then stood even closer while the two of them gazed down at her in her cot as her eyelids finally closed in sleep.

'This is how I wanted it to be,' Luke whispered as his

arm slid around her shoulders. 'A home full of laughter and the sound of children.'

Cassie was overwhelmingly aware of the warmth and strength of his body close to hers but managed to murmur her agreement. Basically, it was what she'd always longed for, too, but with one vital extra ingredient—a husband who loved her.

It was tantalising to stand there beside Luke and imagine that her dreams had come true, but she couldn't afford to give in to hopeless fantasy. It would be far better if she concentrated on what she *could* have.

'I meant to pull my bed out before I put Jenny to sleep,' she murmured as she regretfully slid out from under his arm. How was it that the absence of its warm weight could make her feel suddenly lonely?

'Do it later, Cassie,' he suggested as he caught her hand and stopped her walking away. 'I need to talk to you.'

His serious tone of voice and the expression on his face made her insides tighten with apprehension in spite of the fact that he held onto her hand.

She expected him to lead the way downstairs but instead he led her next door into his own bedroom. He sat on the side of the bed and patted the space beside him with his free hand.

'Join me,' he invited softly, giving a little tug for encouragement. 'We seem to have been tiptoeing around things for ever and I think it's time we cleared the air a bit.'

The unexpected intimacy of sitting beside him on the bed was tempered with a feeling of dread. He looked far too serious for this to be a light-hearted conversation.

'I should have put my cards on the table right from the start,' he said after a brief silence. 'It wasn't fair to you, but at the time I was so worried about the Paynes' threat to take Jenny away that everything else took second place.'

'But you told me all about that,' Cassie pointed out with a puzzled frown. 'That was the reason you asked me to marry you.'

'Not entirely,' he admitted grimly. 'There were other considerations. Things that I didn't tell you about in case...'

She was intrigued but kept silent, guessing from the troubled expression on his face that it was better to leave him to find the words in his own time.

'I know we're not supposed to speak ill of the dead, but it's important to me that there aren't any secrets between us,' he announced suddenly. 'I only went out with Sophie once, and we got caught up in a group celebrating the end of their exams. I don't know whether she'd planned it, but even when the evening degenerated into a glorified pub crawl she insisted we stay with her friends.'

He shrugged fatalistically. 'I was certain that I hadn't drunk more than a couple of pints but the next thing I remembered was waking up and finding her in bed with me. When she told me a few weeks later that she was pregnant...'

Cassie had cringed when Luke had started talking about Sophie, dreading to hear about how much he'd loved his wife. To find out the truth was a shock, but it did ease some of the dreadful disappointment she'd been feeling ever since he'd apparently preferred her colleague.

Not that it meant that he would have fallen in love with her even if Sophie hadn't become pregnant. It was just that Luke, being sort of person he was, once he'd known about the baby he would have insisted on doing the honourable thing to give her his name.

'That's so sad,' she whispered, barely aware that she

was voicing her thoughts aloud. 'You wanted a house full of love and laughter and instead you've ended up with two marriages of convenience.'

'Actually, that's what I wanted to talk about,' he said. 'I want to end our agreement.'

Cassie was certain that her heart stopped beating. That was the *last* thing she'd expected him to say.

'But...but you haven't got custody of Jenny yet,' she faltered, shock dulling her thought processes. 'Have...have I done something wrong?'

'No, Cassie, of course you haven't. Far from it,' he said. 'If it hadn't been for your generosity I doubt that Jennywren would be sleeping in the other room at this moment. I would probably still be trying to trick my way into seeing her at the Paynes' house.'

'Then...then why do you want me to go?' His glowing testimonial wasn't enough to erase the pain of his announcement. She'd always known that this sham marriage of theirs was due to end at some time but she'd still hoped that it would last long enough for her to have a chance to change his mind.

'I *don't* want you to go,' he said fiercely, trapping her trembling hands in his and gripping them tightly. His eyes seemed to glow with a steely light and she was unable to look away. 'The last thing I want is to lose you.'

'But you said—'

'I said I wanted to end our agreement, but I certainly don't want to end our marriage...unless you want to?'

'I don't understand.' She shook her head, as if that would clear her muddled thoughts.

'After I heard you talking to Sophie's mother I thought that this would be easy,' he muttered half under his breath. 'Obviously I'm not making myself clear enough so I'll begin again.'

To her surprise, he slid off the bed beside her to kneel at her feet, both her hands held firmly in his as he met her startled gaze.

'Cassie Thornton, will you do me the honour of becoming my wife?'

Cassie could hardly meet his eyes, more confused than ever. 'But, Luke, we're already married.'

'Not really married,' he pointed out softly as he lifted her chin with one gentle finger until their gazes meshed. 'Not married the way I want to be married to you—"till death us do part",' he quoted.

Cassie stared at him, almost too afraid to breathe let alone answer. She knew she could never be his one and only but it almost sounded as if he was offering her everything she'd always wanted. Surely there must be a catch.

'Why, Luke?' she demanded with a quiver in her voice, the hot press of tears threatening. It was too sudden and too much for her to cope with easily. 'I mean, why have you changed your mind?'

'I haven't, Cassie,' he said softly. 'It's what I've wanted from the first time I met you.'

'What?' she gasped. The fervent words were difficult to accept, so different from everything she'd believed for so long.

'It's true, Cassie,' he said earnestly. 'I fell for you that first day and if I hadn't been such a fool—'

'Don't say that,' she cautioned, in spite of the fact that her heart was bouncing around inside her chest. 'Just think. If you hadn't gone out with Sophie then you wouldn't have your precious Jennywren. Would you really wish her gone?'

'Of course not.' He smiled wryly. 'You always seem

to be able to find something good in a situation, but you still haven't given me an answer. What's it to be?'

It was the lingering apprehension in his eyes that told her how much her answer mattered, and something tight and hard around her heart melted away.

'Oh, Luke,' she sighed, caught halfway between tears and laughter. 'I've loved you since the first day we met, and even though I told myself that your marriage changed everything it didn't—it couldn't. You were the first man I'd ever loved. My one and only, in spite of the fact you'd married someone else.'

'That's the same way I felt about you,' he murmured as he joined her on his bed. He wrapped her in loving arms and drew her down to lie beside him. 'You were the person I'd been waiting for all my life and then, through my own stupidity...' He shook his head as he gazed down into her face, his eyes travelling over each feature as if he wanted to devour her. 'I can't believe that I've been lucky enough to get a second chance.'

Cassie watched in wonder as his head tilted towards hers, hardly able to believe that this was really happening. Then his lips touched hers, a fleeting touch and then another, as though he could hardly believe it either.

Cassie spared a brief thought for the sleeping child in the next room and the tangled path that had brought the three of them together, but by then fleeting touches weren't enough for either of them and the outside world ceased to exist.

'I want to make a new agreement,' Luke growled in her ear long, loving hours later.

They'd had two years of love to catch up on and neither of them had wanted to waste precious time in sleep. Now they were lying wrapped in each other's arms while they waited for Jenny to wake at the start of a brand new day.

'A new agreement?' Cassie echoed as she continued to run a loving hand up and down the long, lean length of Luke's back, revelling in her new freedom to touch the man she'd loved so long.

'Ooh, yes,' he groaned in a mixture of agony and ecstasy as he arched like a big lazy cat. 'Let's agree that you'll continue doing that on a daily basis for the rest of our lives.'

Cassie chuckled. That certainly wouldn't be a hardship for her. She loved touching every ridge and hollow of his powerful body.

'And in return?' she bargained as she scraped fingertips lightly over smooth warm skin and felt him shiver in response. 'What will you do for me?'

'Anything you want,' he promised recklessly.

'Anything?' She heard the sultry tone in her own voice and grinned when she realised just how much she had changed in the last few hours. This was certainly a new Cassie to the one who'd kept her emotions hidden.

'Anything,' he agreed huskily as one broad palm slid over her ribs in search of the soft weight of a naked breast.

In seconds Cassie was doing some purring of her own and was just beginning another voyage of exploration when the outside world intruded with the harsh ring of the doorbell.

Luke groaned.

'Who on earth can that be at this time of the morning? Don't they realise that some people have got some serious loving to catch up on?'

Cassie looked across at the alarm clock on the bedside

cabinet as he leapt out of bed and scrambled to find some clothes, and she chuckled.

'Jenny obviously appreciates the fact that we wanted a lazy morning. Perhaps producing those teeth has worn her out. It's gone nine and she hasn't demanded attention yet.'

'Unlike our visitor,' Luke pointed out darkly as the bell pealed again.

There was an answering squeak from Jenny's room and Cassie had to stop ogling Luke's semi-clothed body to find some clothes of her own.

They reached the bedroom door together as the bell rang a third time, but Luke paused long enough to pull her dressing-gown-clad body into his arms for a gentle kiss.

'You do believe that I love you?' he whispered as he cupped her cheeks and gazed intently into her eyes.

'Of course I do,' she said, the words coming straight from her heart without a trace of doubt. 'And I love you, too.'

There was no time to say more as they hurried off in opposite directions, Luke to deal with their impatient visitor and Cassie to attend to an equally impatient Jenny.

She'd barely had time to wash and change her little charge, ready for her belated breakfast, when Luke called from downstairs.

'Cassie, could you come here for a minute?'

The request was very ordinary but suddenly a shiver passed over her as though some hidden danger threatened her new-found happiness. There was something in his voice that told her not to take the time to don her own clothes, that it was important to hurry downstairs straight away.

The first person she saw as she entered the sitting room was Mrs Payne, standing stiffly in the middle of the room, and her arms tightened reflexively around the precious youngster who had already found a special place in her heart.

'Mrs Payne,' she said breathlessly, feeling the slow sweep of heat up into her face as the older woman eyed her from tousled head to bare feet. 'I didn't think you were coming to collect Jenny until tomorrow.'

'I wasn't,' she agreed bluntly. 'But we received some information this morning and I didn't think it could wait.'

Her expression was stony and it sent a spear of dread through Cassie's heart.

They couldn't lose Jenny. Not now. She'd been the reason Luke had proposed the marriage they'd both wanted and now that they'd discovered their love for each other it would be a tragedy if they were to lose the child they both loved.

'Would you like to sit down?' Cassie gestured towards the settee as Luke stood grimly silent in front of the window. His expression was unreadable but his feelings were revealed by the white knuckles across each of his tightly fisted hands.

'That won't be necessary. What I have to say won't take long, but you both need to know,' Mrs Payne said shortly, then turned to speak to Luke. 'We have received incontrovertible proof that Jenny is not your daughter. We have a sworn statement that her father is another of the doctors at St Augustine's—a married man—and that she deliberately set out to trap you. When we supply the information to the court, will you drop your claim for custody?'

There was barely time for a single heartbeat between the shocking news and Luke's answer.

'Certainly not,' he said swiftly, his jaw set at a pugnacious angle. 'I don't care what legal or medical documents you can produce, Jennywren's my daughter in all the ways that matter. I took on a lifetime's responsibility for her when I married Sophie and nothing has changed that.'

'Don't you care that she was fathered by another man? That she doesn't share your blood?' the older woman demanded with a swift glance in Jenny's direction, her amazement overriding her embarrassment at the sordid topic.

'I couldn't care less whose blood she shares,' he declared quietly as he walked over to Cassie and lifted a subdued Jenny into his arms. 'I already loved her before she was born and nothing you've told me has changed that. Jenny is *my* daughter and I'll fight you through every court in the country if I have to to keep her.'

For several long moments the only sound in the room was Jenny's gurgle of delight as she explored the buttons on the front of Luke's partially closed shirt.

Cassie's heart was so full of pride that she didn't know whether to laugh or cry. If she'd ever needed proof that Luke was completely different to her own parents she'd just received it.

She'd always known that he was special, but this made him a man in a million. Now everything depended on Mrs Payne's response.

'I see,' she said softly, and Cassie saw a new vulnerability behind the stiffly proper exterior. 'And if my husband and I agreed to allow you full custody, would you want to shut us out of her life?'

'Certainly not,' Cassie answered swiftly, knowing that, for all her abrasiveness, the older woman was desperate not to lose this last contact with her only child. 'Every little girl deserves to be spoiled by at least one set of grandparents.'

'Provided those grandparents also promise to spoil any brothers and sisters as they come along,' Luke added as he wrapped a supportive arm around Cassie's shoulders. 'After all, love isn't something that you have to share out. It just grows bigger and bigger the more people you have to love.'

A smile crept over Mrs Payne's face, the first truly genuine smile Cassie could remember seeing there.

'Now I'm certain that Sophie knew what she was doing when she married you,' she said quietly. 'I don't approve of the way she tricked you into the marriage but she couldn't have chosen a better father for her baby.'

As if Jenny understood what they were all talking about, she suddenly squealed and patted Luke's cheek with a pudgy hand before planting a noisy kiss there.

'That seems to make it unanimous!' Cassie said through their shared laughter.

'In which case, I'll leave the three of you to get on with your day,' Mrs Payne offered. 'We'll sort out a convenient time to bring the rest of her things over.'

'Don't forget, you'll need to keep her cot for when she comes to visit,' Luke said, obviously prepared to be generous now that the tension had gone.

'Thank you. We'll do that,' she said with gratitude in every syllable. 'But perhaps we'll wait until she's finished teething. I think we're a bit too old to want to go through all that again,' she added honestly, then made her farewells.

'Oh, Luke!' Cassie exclaimed, barely able to take in the momentous events of the last half-hour. 'She's yours! Jenny's all yours at last!'

'*Ours*,' he corrected as he tightened his arm around her and formed a loving circle about the three of them. 'She's ours.'

Cassie wrapped one arm around his waist and the other around Jenny and revelled in the feeling of completion. This was where she had always longed to be and her dreams had finally come true.

Jenny squealed and grabbed hold of a fistful of Cassie's hair and tried to stuff it in her mouth.

'Uh-oh! It looks like it's time to feed our little monster before she eats us,' Luke said with a laugh.

'At least she doesn't seem to be bothered by her teeth any more. She didn't disturb us once in the night.'

Luke slanted her a wicked look as he strapped Jenny securely in her chair.

'How long will it be before she's due for a nap?' he asked as he reached for a banana, much to Jenny's delight.

'Not for several hours yet. Why?' She busied herself with mashing some of the fruit and offering the first spoonful to the waiting mouth.

'I was just wondering how long it would be before we could get to work on our next project,' he said innocently.

'Next project?' Was there more decorating to do?

'Well, I did make Mrs Payne promise she would spoil Jenny's brothers and sisters so I thought we ought to get started on a playmate for her as soon as possible. After all, if there are two of them they can keep each other company while we're otherwise occupied.'

He swooped to plant a noisy kiss on Jenny's cheek then a more lingering one on Cassie's lips.

'I don't know,' she said breathlessly when he lifted his head. 'I don't think Jenny's quite old enough to babysit, yet, but the idea of working on a brother or sister for her sounds interesting.'

She threw him a saucy grin over her shoulder as she

spooned the next mouthful between little white teeth, her heart full to the brim with happiness.

'So?' he prompted, his blue eyes full of wicked temptation.

Cassie drew in a quivering breath, still hardly able to believe that this man, her one and only love, was hers for ever. Then she saw his loving expression and knew it was true.

'So,' she said softly, huskily, drawing each word out. 'When she goes down for her nap, I just might let you persuade me...'